IF

SHE

WERE

BLIND

AFTER TWELVE SERIES, BOOK ONE

Laney Wylde

Wylde

IF SHE WERE BLIND
Copyright ©2018 Laney Wylde
All rights reserved.
Printed in the United States of America
First Print Edition: March 2019

WWW.CRIMSONTREEPUBLISHING.COM

SUMMARY: Not everyone can get justice the traditional way—that's where Estlyn Collins comes in. A young lawyer in Santa Monica, her "legal" service, After Twelve, works outside the courts to tip the scales of justice…for a price. Estlyn's success rate is stellar and she's on top of it all, but when she's contacted by a ghost from her past seeking vengeance against her, she's shaken to her very core…

ISBN: 978-1-63422-338-6 (paperback)
ISBN: 978-1-63422-339-3 (e-book)
Cover Design by: Marya Heidel
Typography by: Courtney Knight
Editing by: Cynthia Shepp

Fiction / Romance / New Adult
Fiction /Thrillers / Legal
Fiction / Romance / Multicultural & Interracial
Fiction / Romance / Contemporary

For Ethan.

LADIES WHO PLAY WITH FIRE MUST REMEMBER
THAT SMOKE GETS IN THEIR EYES.

~Mae West

ONE

Estlyn

I SLIDE THE ENVELOPE across the table, careful to avoid the condensation ring left by Sean's whiskey on ice. He stares down at the black *(12)* on the upper right corner, then lifts his head and rolls his eyes. Good. He has heard of us.

"I'm not interested in whatever you think you have in here." Sean shoves it back toward me before he stands in that pompous way famous assholes like him do—straightening his jacket, ducking his chin to pretend he doesn't want anyone to recognize him, then looking around hoping someone does. Always basking in the spotlight. Always too big to fall.

Except he's not. I mean, physically. On his feet, he's short. These stars always seem like they'll be tall, but they are often smaller than they appear on screen.

Right now, he's puny.

My fingers intertwine, and I glare up at him through my eyebrows. These precious seconds

1

are my favorite of any meeting—the moment after the scale tips but before the prick in front of me knows it's no longer in his favor.

"No problem, I'm sure the state will place Micah in a good home."

He pauses, the fingertips of his right hand lingering on the table's surface.

"The first foster home I went to was," I continue. "My new parents tried to hide the fact that they weren't interested in taking care of an eleven-year-old, especially one who looked like me." Tilting my head, I narrow my eyes on Sean. "Luckily, their teenage son had a thing for 'dark girls with tight pussies.' I'm sure Micah will find a foster brother or sister to fondle him just like I did."

Crashing into the booth in front of me, he hisses, "What do you want?"

I nod toward the manila envelope he has yet to open. He huffs as he tears into it, then sifts through the evidence I've compiled linking him to his bastard son, the mother of whom is an undocumented immigrant. Deporting her would be a breeze, and God knows Sean won't want the inconvenience of raising his child.

"After what you did to Samson's client, I thought for sure you wouldn't mind your son having an older friend to play naked games with."

He glowers at me and sighs. "Client?"

"You've sexually assaulted more than one

of your backup dancers? It's that hard to keep track?" When he refuses to answer, I continue, "Denise Arden wants her job back and a twenty-percent raise."

He scoffs. "We replaced her."

"I know," I sympathize. "I don't know why she wants to work for her rapist, but she insisted."

"If this is about the money, I can pay—"

"Your hush money? No, I'm afraid she doesn't want any more of that."

"She signed an NDA. Legally, I should get that money back now."

"Now that I know you raped her?" I smile in response to his silent fuming. "No, she's in compliance with her NDA. She wasn't the only one who knew what you did to her. Next time, pay off all the people you harass." He's drumming his fingers on the table. Buying time. Searching for a way out of this. I spread my elbows to the left and right, then lean toward him. My voice low, I ask, "What was your favorite part? How she tasted? When she said 'no?' That made you hard, huh, when she *didn't* want it? Did you like it when she begged you to stop? Did you fire her when she quit resisting? When it wasn't fun anymore?"

His words are cold when he says, "She got boring. All of them do when they think they're too good to get on their knees for the job."

"Well…" I sit back, then pull a packet of paper

from my bag. "She won't be boring now, will she?"

His lips twist into a smirk. "No. I suppose she won't."

I hand him the contract Denise and I drafted. "If you'd be so kind as to sign this. Please initial all the highlighted portions. Denise's agent will be in touch, and you'll never hear from me again." I watch as he does, then snap pictures of each page once he returns them.

As he straightens from the table and smooths the buttons of his shirt, I say, "You know, you should always read what you sign."

Into my shirt, I ask, "That should be enough to start, right?"

The plainclothes police officers in the booth behind me start toward Sean. The woman pulls handcuffs from her jacket pocket. Sean shouts over her while she reads him his rights, "I didn't confess to anything. What the fuck is this?"

I hold my phone up and take another photo, this one of him getting arrested. Then I read from the page he signed, "'I, the undersigned, confess to forcibly raping Denise Arden on multiple occasions from the start of her employment in May 2017 to her dismissal...' It goes on from there." I tap on my phone. "And now *TMZ* knows."

"They can't make any of this stick."

I shrug. "We really don't care."

And we don't. It just takes one—one survivor—to step up and accuse a star of sexual misconduct, one domino to tip and knock the rest over. His other victims will come forward in the upcoming months. As long as his career is over, we don't care if the police lock him up or not.

Once I snatch the envelope of blackmail from the floor, I tuck it into my bag. I know what Denise requested, but I just can't let the police have Micah's mom. If they want her gone, they'll figure it out themselves. My head ducks toward my chest when I scoot past the cops on my way to the exit. I'm not a fan of collaborating with the police, but Denise insisted. And I give my clients what they ask for—holistic justice.

Denise signed a nondisclosure agreement when she and her crackpot lawyer sat with Sean's attorney. Money was exchanged—the amount, of course, she couldn't tell me. Why they paid her, she, again, couldn't disclose. I asked instead for a list of friends, family, and coworkers who could tell her story to me. I didn't need the whole truth, just enough to make him squirm.

She has her holistic justice. I have my thirty grand. Or most of it.

On my way out of the strip club, I message Denise from my Google number specific to her case: *Without a hitch. LAPD have him in custody. Please wire remaining funds.*

She replies within the minute. *Funds transferred. Thank you.*

Now I have my thirty grand. I don't usually

charge so much, but I showed my face to a high-profile target and the police. Plus, she'll get that money back—and then some—in her civil suit.

There's a bar two blocks away. I know because I've worked a surprising number of cases at this club. Bentley's Dive is something of a gem. It's quiet and lit well enough to know how much regret I'll feel in the morning over the one-night stand I meet there.

I never spend the night alone after I meet a target in person, which I rarely do. It's impossible to know who can find me despite the security in my building and the fake names I do business under. I don't have a boyfriend or roommate, and the guard puppy the humane society told me was an Akita mix grew up to be a medium-sized dog that would sooner roll over for an intruder than bite him. The humane society does not take kindly to returns, but they do take them. So, besides me, my apartment is empty.

But I'm not going to sleep if it stays empty tonight.

I'm relieved to see an open stool at the bar. When I hop onto it, a sandy-haired guy in rolled-up sleeves places his palms on the counter and leans toward me. "What can I get for you?"

I study his face a moment, taking in his green eyes and splatter of freckles over his cheekbones. "You're new." Maybe I frequent this bar too… frequently.

He pushes off the bar. "Yeah. Do you want a drink?"

"Old fashioned." I put my hand out. "Wait, have you learned how to make one of those?"

He glowers as he thumps the squat tumbler against the bar. "Ice?"

I nod. "What's your name?"

"Cal," he answers without looking up from the glass.

"Kal, as in Superman?"

He shrugs. "It's a nickname."

"What's your real name?"

"Linus."

"Wow, your parents must hate you."

He snickers. "You have no idea." He tips his chin. "What's your name?"

"Estlyn."

"After E. E. Cummings?"

"Who?" I wink.

Cal coats the rim of the glass with the orange peel, then drops it in my drink. "ID."

I reach into my messenger bag, then pass him my driver's license.

"Estlyn Collins?" He raises an eyebrow.

"I prefer just Estlyn, like Zendaya or Beyoncé."

"What's your address?"

I rattle off the phony North Hollywood address I have memorized.

"Mm-hmm, and your birthday?"

I give him that, too. It's only one day different

from my real one.

"Where's your real ID?"

"Excuse you, asshole, that is my real ID."

He shakes his head as he bends the card back and forth. "You look like you're nineteen."

"So why would I have my ID say I'm twenty-five if I only needed to be twenty-one? That's too big a lie to get away with."

"Or is it the perfect lie?"

"Look, I have a law degree and a six-figure salary. I'm probably older than you." I reach for the drink, but he picks it up and steps back from the bar. "Don't you have other customers to not serve?"

"Where's your degree from?"

"UCLA."

Cal clicks his tongue. "Ooh… wrong answer." He finally passes me my drink and my license.

"Aw, you went to USC, didn't you?" He nods as I take a sip. "Do you think that's why you're behind the bar and I passed it?"

"Can I interest you in a table over there?" He points behind me. "Or the door?"

I shed my jacket, revealing the low-cut top beneath. "Can I interest you in a night of no-strings-attached fucking?"

I expect him to be taken aback by my abrupt change in subject, but he responds in kind. "Sure. Do you have a less-bitchy friend?"

I lean my chest against the counter to press

my less-than-ample breasts together. "What if I don't talk the rest of the night? Except, of course, to cry out 'Linus' during climax."

"It's Cal."

"Sure…" I shrug, "I could scream 'Cal' instead."

"I have a girlfriend."

"Ah." I twist the glass between my fingers. "Can you point me in the direction of someone less romantically entangled or more morally creative?"

Sighing, Cal ignores me and nods to the customer two seats away. "Another?" he asks.

Sipping my drink, I rotate to scan the bar for someone single and worthy of my utmost disrespect, but it's a Tuesday night. It's not exactly packed in here. While I wait for the right guy to walk in, I pull my business card from my wallet. It's an uncomplicated design—a white background with a black *(12)* on the front and my work email on the back. With a pen, I write, *listen: there's a hell of a good universe next door*. I swallow the rest of my drink, then secure the card and a twenty under the glass before getting up.

After I cross the room, I claim the booth Cal pointed toward before I propositioned him, then relax as I scroll through my email for prospective cases. About half my inquiries usually concern infidelity, and this batch in my inbox is no different. Since I'm in the revenge business, I get a lot of requests to mutilate philandering dicks, though I have yet to take a machete to someone's crotch. Really, is that the most clever way to screw someone over for screwing around?

Also, I operate (mostly) within the law. Because I'm a lawyer, I know that the law is a beautiful and fluid concept created to be twisted to fit my client's needs. So, no, I've never accepted ten grand to castrate someone. But I have accepted fifteen to dismantle a cheater's life brick by slimy brick.

I skim the bolded subject lines of the unread messages until the inquiry from this morning constricts my airways again. It's not bold anymore. I've read it at least a dozen times, the name of the sender more than a hundred. I should reply. I have to. Because if he doesn't go to me for revenge, he'll go somewhere else.

"Your change." I look up from my phone. Cal drops a few dollars and a receipt on my table.

After I fold the bills, I hand them back. "You need this more than I do, what with that enormous debt from your second-rate alma mater."

He rolls his eyes, huffing as his fingers comb back his dirty-blond hair. Still, he doesn't turn down the cash. Picking up the receipt, I read the bottom. Cal had scribbled the rest of the E. E. Cummings quote I'd started on my card: *let's go*. I flip the receipt over to find he wrote, *Shift ends at 10:00. I prefer you scream "Linus."* –

TWO

Cal

"WHAT DO YOU DO again?" I ask Estlyn as she flicks on the light in her apartment. It's clean and sparse as if she just moved in or is about to move out. No sign of a roommate. No pictures on the walls or wedding invitations on the fridge. I wander into the living room to see if she has a view of the water her building is on. It's dark, but it's there.

She shrugs off her jacket, revealing the flawless mocha skin of her shoulders. "I'm a lawyer."

"For the mob?" I chuckle, but now I'm actually worried she is. She's young and rich with a diagnosable level of hubris. And her ID *was* a fake. This apartment is in Santa Monica, not North Hollywood. I'm not even sure her name is Estlyn. And who verbally abuses a bartender and then invites him over for a fuck in the same breath?

...And what idiot says yes?

Estlyn heads behind the kitchen counter, then opens the refrigerator. "Which mob?" She glances over her shoulder. "Can I get you anything to drink?"

I step on my heels to slip out of each shoe. "Water is fine." She hands me a bottle before resting her elbows on the counter. Her shirt is slinky enough that I can see beyond her cleavage to just above her navel. There is no bra to obstruct my view.

"You don't need to be drunk to cheat on your girlfriend with a stranger?"

My eyes skim her long neck to her dark eyes. "We broke up a month ago." So maybe that's why I said yes. Maybe I've been feeling like shit. Maybe I needed a win after I walked in on another guy's bare ass writhing on top of my girlfriend in our bed. And it was a *hairy* ass—think shag carpet after a perm. That's the only consolation I have.

"Amicably?"

I shake my head.

"How long were you together?"

"Five years."

Her eyes squint in suspicion. "How old are you?"

"Twenty-four."

"You ever had meaningless sex before?"

I shake my head again. "You?" I don't know why I'm asking. Clearly, hookups are routine for her.

I'm surprised when she says, "No." Even more surprised when I believe her. She looks nervous now. No, ashamed. Her hands move to her face to cover the crimson rising to her cheeks, but she tucks her wavy hair behind her ears instead.

After I set my water on the counter, I round the corner toward her. I tip her chin up until her eyes meet mine. My thumb reflexively runs along the silky skin of her jaw. "Why now?"

Estlyn whispers, "I promised not to talk." Her fingers hook into my belt loops, then pull me to her.

She keeps her word. Her breaths and moans are wordless until, sweating and clutching the top of her headboard, she gasps my name. No one has ever said my name like that—with that intensity, that hunger. Not even my ex.

And never *Linus*.

Not that my ex said *Cal* often. Now I know why.

Estlyn's grip on the headboard loosens, her forehead rolling against the wood as her lungs calm. Her eyes close, her skin glistening in the light sneaking through the window. The sweaty skin of her chest presses into mine as she relaxes against me. But I don't want her to.

I need her to say it again.

Shifting her off me, I push her onto her back before dropping the used condom into the trash can by the bed. Her thighs are parted when my fingers and mouth find their way between them. Goose bumps rise up her slender waist all the way to her throat. I hear her say my name again, the syllables sharp and breathy, tense, then relieved.

Leaning over, I grab a condom from where she'd left them on the bedside table. I roll it on, then enter her again. She wraps her legs around my waist, burying her face in my neck. The dewy skin on my jaw heats and chills with each breath she gasps against it. I slide my hands under her back to press her flush against me. Each thrust compels my name from her lungs, crescendoing until she screams *"Linus!"* then exhales another ragged "Linus" as I throb inside her.

I lie next to her, our feet tangled in the pillows at the head of the bed. My arms hold her close, my lips tasting her temple. I'm not sure why she lets me. We both know it's over.

My eyes shut so I don't have to watch it end.

THREE

Estlyn

My sheets still smell like Linus when I wake. I didn't even put clothes on after the second time we had sex. Or third? It's all blurry now that the alcohol is leaving my system. I push up from my pillow to see a cup of coffee and a note on my nightstand.

i like my body when it is with your body. It is so quite new a thing.

What is with this guy and E. E. Cummings?

Wait, is Linus still here? I scramble out of the bed, pull on a T-shirt and panties from my dresser, then take the coffee out to the kitchen. Scanning my small apartment and out the sliding-glass doors to the balcony, I realize he's gone. I sigh, relieved I don't have to face my first one-night stand in the unforgiving light of day.

Yes, my *first* one-night stand. When I said I didn't sleep alone after face-to-face target encounters, I meant I usually crashed at my brother's house. But he just got married. And they're trying to get pregnant. Loudly. With lots of dirty talk. From my brother. It's somehow even more disturbing than I can describe.

I sip my coffee, but it's not hot anymore. After I pop it in the microwave, I hop onto the counter to scroll through my email while I wait. Just one new case request since last night. The subject: *Please Help: Out of Options*. Hell yes. An excuse to ignore the ticking bomb below it.

The body of the email is short and reticent:

Samson,

My daughter was the victim of an illegal act at the hands of an A-list actor. The court acquitted him, and she lost her job and was publicly humiliated in the process. Our lawyer told us that we have exhausted all of our legal options, but he gave me your card.

Can you help?
Lola Sanchez

These are the types of cases I love. Not the ones where there are no legal options because nothing illegal was done, but where there are no legal options left because it's the rich and powerful against the unconnected and nameless. I reply immediately.

Ms. Sanchez,

My assistant will meet with you today at Milo Olive in Santa Monica at 1:00.
Please bring a fifty-percent deposit of $15,000, along with all relevant legal materials for our review.
We look forward to the opportunity to work with you.

Justice always,
Samson

Since these last-hope cases are risky and time-intensive, I tend to take on only one of them at a time. The microwave beeps, and I retrieve my coffee. I take it and the phone to the balcony, where I select two cheating cases from my inbox and offer consultations for tomorrow and Monday. To the remaining eight, I send a form response telling them I will reach out as soon as I have availability. I leave the bomb to count down.

When I started the embryo of this business thirteen years ago, I never dreamed I would have so much work I'd have to turn some down. I also never imagined I could make my living at it.

I was eleven the first time the justice system failed me, and I was twelve the first time I realized I could do something about it. What I'd said to Sean about the biological son of my foster parents raping me was the truth. But after what had happened to my family, I'd known my place. No one would have taken my word over Brock's. So, I'd shut my eyes and thighs and prayed every night he wouldn't do it. But every night he had.

It was when my foster family took in Rory that I decided not to give a fuck about my place. Rory was barely nine, new to the system, and the cutest, quietest redhead I had ever met. When I found blood on the toilet seat after the little boy left the bathroom one night, it was obvious what Brock was doing to him. There was no way in hell I was going to let Rory live like that.

So, I did what any rational seventh grader would do—I framed Brock for plotting a school shooting. It'd been easy, really. Because it was May, he had a current high school yearbook. I found who had signed it and included them in a manifesto, typed by Brock, then shared it in one of those chat rooms for aspiring psychopaths. I'd made sure to print one out for good measure. It was all done on the family computer, which was password-protected with my foster parents' anniversary—the same password as the combination to the gun safe in the garage.

Since I didn't have any gloves to keep my prints off the incriminating evidence, I put my hands in quart-size plastic bags and carefully removed a handgun from the safe. I pinched it between my index finger and thumb, holding it away from me like it could go off at any time. It was light, so I doubted it was loaded, but guns scared the shit out of me, so I took precautions. I slid the gun and printed manifesto into a hidden inside pocket of Brock's backpack.

The next morning just before homeroom, I went to my principal's office and asked to speak to someone—*anyone*—about an emergency that had happened at home. A counselor ushered me into her window-walled office, where I blurted out, "My foster brother took a gun to school today, but he told me he'd shoot me if I told anyone." Her eyes grew wide as she picked up her desk phone and asked what school he went to. Long story short, Brock was arrested, Rory and I were removed from that home immediately, and Brock's parents were permanently disqualified as foster parents.

That afternoon, Rory and I sat in our foster agency's office, each with our trash bag of belongings. He was shaking, scared, and playing brave. When I reached out and took his hand, he wept.

Rory and I were placed into the same emergency foster home. Around midnight, he crept into my room and told me he couldn't sleep. He lay down next to me and whispered, "When do you think I'll get to go home?"

I shrugged. "I don't know, Ror. What are you

in for?"

"I don't know. My mom left a while ago, and she never came home."

I froze. If his mom abandoned him and no family had claimed him yet, his chances of getting out of the system were nonexistent. Instead of giving him false hope, I lied. "I'm sure she misses you."

"Do you think they'll let us live in the same house? Me and you? Until my mom comes to get me?"

Oh God, could he break my heart more? "Of course, Ror. I'll do whatever I can to stay with you." He smiled. "Now, go to bed. No one's going to hurt you here. But if they do, I'll take care of it, okay?"

He'd trusted me as he left my room that night. I had never had that before—the responsibility of someone's trust. I wasn't ever going to break it.

It wasn't until eighth grade that I realized I could monetize my form of vigilante justice. I noticed a girl in my history class was being cyberbullied by a bunch of flat-ass bitches on Instagram. Hannah and I were both loners—me being the foster kid with a dad in prison, her being the academically enthusiastic band geek. Oh, and she had a stutter. Poor thing. I passed her a note in third period, asking if I could meet her at lunch. She was so excited someone wanted to eat lunch with her that her response had included five exclamation points. Over mushy cheese pizza and chocolate pudding, I interviewed her about her problem. I then presented her a paper outlining the weaknesses of each member of the clique that had led the attack against her.

"Now," I said, "we can approach this one of two ways. We can go after them or, no offense, we can make you less of a dork."

She flashed her braces at me. "None taken."

"Okay." I pointed to the page with the tip of my pencil. "Alma is the leader of the hive. She has, like, a *serious* crush on Wyatt Galaway. He's a freshman."

"Ooh…"

"And Alma has been bragging about the fact that he's going to ask her to winter formal." High school dances were as elusive as the Academy Awards for middle-schoolers. "But, I'm betting for the right price, I could get him to ask you." The right price because Wyatt was one of the few popular kids who wasn't rich, just good-looking and athletic.

She didn't miss a beat before eagerly asking, "How much?"

"I'll have to find out. First, you'll have to try to look sexy. Do you know how to do your hair? Do you have contact lenses? Do you have clothes that fit you?"

She nods. "I can get all of that."

"Great. Try to look cute most days at school,

okay? I'll handle the rest. And look, if he won't ask you, I'll for sure get him to take a cute selfie with you. Make Alma jealous."

Fortunately, Wyatt could be bought. It cost two hundred dollars for Wyatt to take Hannah, and fifty extra to post pictures on Instagram. I took my first client shopping for a dress, styled her hair, and did her makeup for the dance. In foster care, I'd learned all about legal forms and rights to privacy, so I typed up a contract for Wyatt to sign that said he was obligated to keep the payment a secret. He signed it. Hannah paid me four hundred dollars, out of which I paid Wyatt. He got one hundred and twenty-five before the dance and the same amount the following Monday after he posted pictures and kept his mouth shut.

After that, Alma and her minions spewed more hate than ever on the web, calling Hannah a slut and a whore. *Creative.* But none of that mattered. For just four hundred dollars, I had secured Hannah's new status as a high school-dating hottie, and Hannah brought in my first batch of referrals. The beta version of After Twelve was born.

I continued working jobs through high school, creating a mini empire of vengeance. My business earned me enough to buy an almost-new car and start a savings account for college, but I struggled to gain a client base when I moved onto UCLA's campus. I had to start from scratch, and I wasn't used to advertising my services. What was I supposed to do, go up to girls in my dorms and say, *Hey, if someone stabbed you in the back, I'd be happy to stab them back. What's your financial situation? I have Venmo, but prefer cash?* Besides, I had enough savings and grants and scholarships to cover all my expenses, so I let Lady Justice do her job my first two years of college.

Then that bitch took the wrong day off.

MS. SANCHEZ IS ALREADY seated when I arrive at the restaurant. Her fingernails are click-clacking on the table, anxiety radiating from every inch of her. She's beautiful, with warm, caramel skin and dark curls cascading over her shoulders. If I had to guess, I'd say she's only ten years older than I am. No ring. Just a young, single mom whose daughter auditioned for the wrong TV show.

I drop my messenger bag on her table and reach my hand out for hers. "Ms. Sanchez?"

She forces a tight-lipped smile and stands to shake my hand. "Hi, are you—"

"Zoe Whitaker," I lie, using the name I picked for this case. "Samson showed me your inquiry." We sit, and I ask, "Have you had a chance to order?"

She shakes her head. "I'm not hungry."

"What about a drink?"

"Yeah, okay. Thanks."

The waiter stops to take our order as I pull my legal pad from my bag. "How is your daughter holding up, Ms. Sanchez?"

"Uh," she chokes back, "not well."

"I'm sorry to hear that. What's her name?"

"Mia."

I nod and hand her the most important form of any case. "Before we begin, I'll need you to sign this nondisclosure agreement. Anything we discuss cannot be repeated to anyone. If you and Mia talk about this, it cannot be over the phone, via text, or through email. It must be exclusively in person."

She utters a shaky, "Okay," and initials or signs every highlighted portion.

I reach for her hand, briefly squeezing it before taking the contract back. Michael told me once that, in general, I can come across a little horse-decapitate-y... so I try to add a nurturing, feminine touch whenever I can. "Can you explain what happened?"

"Uh, where to start? Have you heard of the show, *When We Fall*?"

"Of course. It's in, what, its second season now?"

She nods. "Mia played Jade. It wasn't a huge role. She wasn't in every episode, but in about half. It was her big break, you know?"

I nod as I jot down notes.

"Taylor East is the lead. He and Mia started dating about six months ago. Not much later, Taylor filmed them..."

She can't stomach the rest of the sentence, so I help her out. "Having sex?"

"Without her knowledge, then posted it on the web."

"Was the sex consensual?"

"Yes. Well, not legally—she's sixteen and he's twenty-seven."

"Okay, and you reported the statutory rape and the video to the police."

"Yes. They charged him with statutory rape and production and distribution of child pornography."

"And who was your DDA?"

"Raphael Ramirez."

I nod. "Did it go to trial?"

"Yes. He was acquitted of all charges."

"Because he claimed he didn't know her age and that she agreed to the filming. It's a he-said, she-said situation, and he's a big star while she's a fledgling actress trying to get publicity to help her career. Crying rape in the industry is in vogue right now, and the judge isn't buying it."

She sighs. "That's exactly why."

I shake my head. "And she was fired?"

"As soon as we filed charges."

"Have you considered suing for wrongful

termination?"

"We are suing the director, yes."

"And your private lawyer recommended Samson?"

"No, Ramirez did."

I drop the pen on the legal pad and sit back. A deputy district attorney knows about After Twelve? And recommended us? Either Ms. Sanchez is wearing a wire, or Ramirez is shady. Or maybe Officer Monroe put him up to this. But he couldn't, right? He couldn't connect me or Michael or Rory to After Twelve.

It doesn't matter why Ramirez recommended me, I decide. I won't be giving them anything to use against me, anyway. "Do you understand what After Twelve does?"

"Not entirely. Ramirez just said that Samson can get justice in a way that the courts can't."

"Legally. We can't castrate Taylor or anything." *In case you're listening, Ramirez.*

She smiles. "Are you sure?"

I return her smile. "Our goal is holistic justice. In other words, not just accountability for the accused, but some form of restitution for the victim. What would you like to see happen to Taylor East?"

"A confession and public apology would be nice."

"Okay."

"Ideally, I'd like an eye for an eye. Ruin his

career and humiliate him like he did to Mia."

"One could accomplish the other," I mutter as I take a note. I glance up at Ms. Sanchez and ask, "And for her?"

"Her agent has booked auditions—something to restore her career and confidence. But, I'm not looking for you to do anything for her."

"Would she be interested in having her role as Jade back if I can get it?"

She shakes her head.

"I'll need to verify the facts of the case and, possibly, meet with Mia."

"Of course."

"If I find that your case against him is solid," I write on my notepad as I instruct her, "we will work out an elegant solution—sans bolt cutters. Because Mia is a victim of child pornography, she will be eligible to sue for restitution from offenders who view her online."

"Even though Taylor isn't paying anything?"

I smirk and add a caustic, "Welcome to the legal system. Though, you *can* sue him in civil court, which I recommend. The restitution is not something I have time to handle, but I recommend you speak to your lawyer or Ramirez about it. Mia should be registered with the federal government to get a notice in the mail each time someone is convicted of downloading or distributing the video East posted." I rip the top page from the pad and hand it to Ms. Sanchez.

"Here is the information for your attorney." I pack the legal pad away in my bag. "Now, the matter of the retainer—"

She stares down at her hands as her fingers twist together on the table. "Have you had success in a case like this before?"

"Ms. Sanchez, After Twelve has a ninety-five-percent success rate. As for a case like your daughter's…" Folding my hands on the table, I breathe out, "A few months ago, a college student hired me to help his girlfriend, who'd been arrested for assault. She claimed she defended herself against a politician who attempted to rape her because he recognized her from child pornography."

Ms. Sanchez grimaces.

"She had already been sentenced, and the police were unable to link him to her images, so he walked. One of my private contractors downloaded malware onto his home and work computers that recorded and sent me his web history. Once the politician downloaded her images, I sent the history to the LAPD through their anonymous-tip site. I'm sure that evidence wasn't used because I obtained it illegally, but it at least gave them probable cause for a warrant. The politician was convicted and had to pay his victim—my client's girlfriend—six figures of restitution. He spent six months in jail, and his career ended."

"Okay." She takes a few moments to work up the nerve to ask her next question, and I give her all the time she needs. "What if you... can't? What if it doesn't work?"

"Justice isn't bound by the law, ma'am. She keeps a ledger. Convicted or acquitted, these men are in the red. Everyone must pay what they owe." That usually gets people to jump in, and it works on her, too.

She sighs. "Is a check okay?" and hands me a security envelope.

I take it. "I won't cash it until I've confirmed that I'll take your case." She also gives me the thick manila envelopes of documents as we stand from the table. "Oh, and who is the director you are suing?"

"Ron Calloway."

I shake her hand and nod. "I'll be in touch shortly."

FOUR

Cal

ELLIOT IS STILL TALKING. I didn't start the conversation. I didn't tell him where I went last night. I haven't said even one word.

"I *told* you the best way to get over Erin was to fuck someone else. How many times did I tell you that? Why did it take you so long?"

I ignore him as I pick up another glass to dry and shelve. When I lost my job and girlfriend and the apartment we'd shared a month ago, Elliot let me crash on his couch. He got me a job at the bar he manages, though it's only twenty hours a week and not enough for me to afford my own couch to crash on.

"Who was she? *How* was she?"

I smirk but don't take my attention from my work.

He punches my arm on his way to the bar. "Fuck you."

I hear him at the counter ask, "What can I get for you?"

"Old Fashioned."

I glance up to see Estlyn's bare elbow poking past Elliot's arm. My gut feels light and my chest heavy until some asshole knees me in the balls with:

"Beer. Dealer's choice."

Elliot moves to get their drinks, and I see the guy beside her. *Beer. Dealer's choice.* God. Be a man. Have an opinion. I step out of their view and creep on Estlyn's interaction with this freckled guy next to her. If they're on a date, she is clearly uninterested. From the tablet and notepad in front of her and the glasses over her eyes, it looks like she brought work.

Shit. They're not on a date. They're *dating.* She had no qualms about having sex with me when she thought *I* had a girlfriend because *she* was cheating on her boyfriend. Now she's bringing him here? To what—parade him in front of me? *Message received. It was one night only.*

I step up to Elliot, taking the bottle of whiskey from him. "I got it."

Estlyn smiles at me. *Smiles.* "Linus, settle an argument between Ror and me."

My eyes tighten on her, then on the wedding ring on *Ror's* finger. Are they married? Or is she just having another night of casual sex with a married man?

"The gender of a baby can't be determined by sex position, right?"

Cold-hearted bitch.

"No," I mumble.

"Ha!" she shouts and points at Ror.

"What? I thought you could slow down the boy sperm by doing it standing up."

Estlyn wrinkles her nose at him. "Who told you that?"

"Olivia."

She cackles and tosses her wild curls to fall on the other side of her head. "She just wants to fuck standing up."

"So, the hot water from the shower doesn't kill off the male swimmers?"

"No!" She buries her face in her hands. "God, I know too much about your baby-making."

Okay, what the hell is this? I set her drink in front of her. "Should I put you guys on the same tab?"

She covers the dumbass's hand with hers. "I better pay. My brother's not supposed to drink while his wife's not allowed to. Oh…" She turns to the guy beside her. "Rory, this is Linus."

She winks, and every muscle in my chest relaxes. What is my problem? One-night stand. I don't even have her phone number. Or her real name.

"He's a USC grad, a fan of poetry, and capable of making at least one drink."

She raises her glass to me before she sips the Old Fashioned I prepared her.

"Linus?" Elliot claps his hand on my shoulder. "Oh…" He takes in every inch of Estlyn. Then he repeats louder, "Oh… Well done, *Linus*."

"I know." Estlyn cuts her gaze through her dark lashes to me. "Lucky bastard."

I shake my head and then Rory's hand. "You can call me Cal." Leaning my elbows on the counter, I dart my eyes between them. Rory is bespeckled and hazel-eyed with strawberry-blond hair. Estlyn's skin is darker and freckle-free, her hair and eyes a rich ebony. There's no way they share both parents. My attention settles on him. "Should I be congratulating you?"

"Not yet," Rory replies. "Liv pees on a stick tomorrow. But thank you." His phone buzzes against the bar. "Hang on." He walks away to answer the call.

The Old Fashioned dangles from Estlyn's fingertips. "So, I think I owe you."

I stretch my hands out on the bar and lean across it. "For?"

"You put out last night, and I didn't even buy you a drink." She simpers and asks, "Don't you feel a bit used?"

I sigh and cross my arms on the counter. "Like a common whore."

"Can I remedy this injustice?"

"I don't think you have a choice."

"I assume you don't want a drink here."

"A correct assumption."

"If I take you to dinner, will I get lucky again?"

Thank God this bar is blocking her view of everything below my waist. I swallow, but my throat is dry. "Depends. Can I order steak?"

"Filet mignon if you'd like. Or lobster. Or both."

"Wow, I was that good?"

"Or that easy. When does your shift end?"

I tap the screen of her tablet for the time. It's only seven.

"Now," Elliot chimes in.

Estlyn and I both turn to him.

"Wednesdays are slow anyway."

What are best friends for? Providing work and time off to get laid.

Rory returns to his barstool, and Estlyn points her thumb at me. "I'm ditching you to have sex." She kisses his cheek, then pats his back.

He tips his beer to his lips with one hand and salutes her with the other, apparently unoffended and unsurprised. I'm not sure how I feel about that.

I round the counter and attempt to pick up the shoulder bag she just packed, but she pulls it from me and shoulders it herself.

"Client files." She smiles and adds, "You can hold the door for me instead."

She drives me to a steakhouse on the water—a place I could hardly afford when I had a real job. "The usual table?" the hostess asks. Estlyn nods and follows the woman to a table with a view of the ocean.

"Is Gino here tonight?" Estlyn asks.

"He should be here soon."

"Wonderful." She flashes a rich and powerful smile, then orders. "Gin martini, wet. Shaken, obviously." She nods to me.

"Water is fine, thank you."

The hostess leaves, and Estlyn's foot finds its way up my calf. "Are you an alcoholic?"

There's a softer way to ask why I'm not drinking, but... "My mom is."

"Ah," she breathes as her toes reach my thigh. "How did a USC grad with an alcoholic mom end up working at a bar?"

I catch her foot in my hands and massage my way up her calf. "I lost my job last month."

"*And* got dumped? You're an unlucky penny, Linus."

"They were related."

"Oh? Were you defecating where you ate?"

I smirk as I run the back of my fingertip over the arch of her foot. She doesn't break my stare, doesn't flinch as I tickle her sole. "My girlfriend slept with my boss for a part in his show."

"You worked in the industry?"

"Writer."

"Did she get the part?"

I nod. "And I lost my job."

"Maybe you should have slept with him, too."

I breathe a sarcastic, "Maybe."

"You're not part of the WGA?"

That's the screenwriters' union. For a moment, I'm astonished she knows about it, but she is a lawyer living in Los Angeles. "Doesn't matter. My contract was the problem."

She pulls her foot away and straightens up. Her expression grows serious and her voice silent as the waitress sets our drinks on the table. "I don't like that," she finally says.

My shoulders raise in apathy. "There's nothing to like or not like. It's just how it is."

"Linus." She shakes her head and tsk-tsks. "It's never 'just how it is.' Give me your contract, and I'll take care of it." She reclines against the back of the booth and strokes the inside of my thigh with her foot until she reaches the bulge inside my left pant leg. Her toe runs along it, back and forth, back and forth until it can't swell any larger.

I close my eyes and press my forehead into my folded hands. "I don't want that job back," I breathe.

"That's not the plan, Linus."

I glance over my fingers at her.

"Do you still like it when I say your name, or did I wear it out last night?"

You'll never wear it out. "I like it."

"Have you decided, or do you need more time?"

I flinch at the sound of the waitress's voice. I've never been so grateful for a long tablecloth in my life.

Without stopping, Estlyn looks at me and asks, "Surf and turf okay?"

I nod because I can't speak without sounding like I'm getting serviced under the table.

"Medium rare?" I nod again. To the waitress, Estlyn says, "Two of those, please." When the waitress walks away, she drops her feet to the floor. "The bathrooms here are private. Want to meet me in the women's when you can stand?"

Is she shitting me? Nope. She's up from the table now, tugging her dress down and taking her bag as she leaves.

I discreetly rearrange my dick in my boxer briefs and follow ten feet behind her. It's not like waiting while she's in there is going help.

FIVE

THIS IS FAR AND away the shittiest writer's contract I've seen. Why did Linus even sign it? I guess if you have USC debt and are a creative type in a saturated market, you take any job you can get. I firmly believe God cursed all artists with tormented minds and few job prospects. That's why I'm glad I'm not one of them. Unfortunately for the guy naked in my bed, there isn't anything legal I can do with this contract.

Fortunately for After Twelve, there's a high-profile contact in the PDF Linus emailed me—Director Ron Calloway, the same director that my client, Mia Sanchez, is suing for wrongful termination. His office number is in the contract, but I'm not interested in that one. I'm interested in the emergency contact listed in Linus's phone.

Linus "Cal" Calloway is the son of son-of-a-bitch Ron Calloway.

I researched Linus after I showered him off me yesterday. He graduated from USC three years ago with a BA in Screenwriting. His ex-girlfriend, Erin Kennedy, is an actress whose new role on *When We Fall* will debut the first episode of season three. And his dad was the one who fired him, I deduce, after Linus caught him slutting it up on Erin.

For how much of that relationship was Erin using Linus to get to Ron? She stayed with him *five* years? My God, there are easier ways to get in a director's pants.

Though I can't very well throw a stone when I'm doing the same.

My one-night stand was serendipitous, as the next day Ms. Sanchez presented me with a need to contact Linus's father directly. I knew when Linus left those two E. E. Cummings lines by my bedside that he'd agree to *at least* one more fuck. I mean, does it get more erotic than E. E. Cummings? Romantic poetry aside, what the hell kind of last name is that? It's wet with sex.

So, I took Rory to Linus's bar a few hours after my meeting with Ms. Sanchez. I gauged his reaction to seeing me with another guy, even one as harmless as Ror. His jealousy couldn't have been clearer if it were written in Sharpie on his forehead. So I asked him out—this time on a date. Dates establish an emotional connection. Earn trust. Even involve conversation about family—the family I need as much filth on as I can get.

It's nearly four in the morning by the time

I have a solid plan for Mia Sanchez's case. It's a few minutes after four when I finally have the courage to reply to the email that's been threatening to explode my inbox for forty-eight hours: *Wrongful Imprisonment*.

To whom it may concern,

I am a former police officer seeking justice after I was arrested five years ago for embezzling money from the LAPD.

A few weeks after I finished temporary desk duty, Internal Affairs interrogated me about an offshore account in my name. The account had $75,000, the same total of money that had gone missing from various accounts within the LAPD over one of the weeks I worked administrative duty.

I did not have an offshore account. When I told them this, they showed me records of the exact times I had logged in on my computer to illegally withdraw funds from LAPD accounts I couldn't possibly have access to. Somehow, I was at my desk at all of these times.

I was convicted and spent four years in prison with men I had put there. In addition, I had to pay over $100,000 in fines and legal fees. My wife has left me. My children won't speak to me. The LAPD is withholding my pension. With a felony on my record, I am unable to get a job.

The person who framed me has destroyed my

life. I hired two private investigators to find the person responsible. Because they could not access the LAPD's network, they do not know for sure; however, they and I have narrowed down the suspects to a small list of enemies I might have made while on the force. The timing of my arrest suggests someone connected to Michael Bishop.

Though I do not have a target solidified, I have heard that your team is the best. I am confident that you will be able to find the one who framed me, destroy him, and clear my name.

I have little in liquid funds but have been approved to refinance my home to pay for your services.

I look forward to hearing from you.
Ted Monroe

If two PIs can't solve this, how the hell does he expect me to? How does he expect *anyone* to? Maybe this inquiry isn't the bomb I thought it was. Monroe is out of connections and resources. If I don't help him get revenge, he may try to hire someone else, but they'll fail. I have to trust that they will.

Mr. Monroe,

Thank you for reaching out. At this time, we are not currently taking on new cases. I apologize for the inconvenience.

Justice always,
Samson

I lock my documents and tablet in my file cabinet before I flick off the kitchen lights. I set Linus's phone back on the nightstand and slip into bed beside him.

"Where'd you go?" he murmurs as he rolls me to his chest.

I rest my head in the relaxed muscle just below his shoulder. "Had to get some work done before the morning."

He nuzzles against me and the pillow. "Do you want me to leave?"

"If you leave, how am I going to wake up with you inside me?"

He laughs, then presses his lips against my hair. "Can I take you to breakfast after?"

I shake my head against him. "Maybe you could pick something up while I get ready. I have an early day tomorrow."

"Perfect."

I close my eyes and breathe in Linus. Not Michael. Which is fine. I'm allowed. Nothing to worry about. At all. I'm going to sleep the sound sleep of a person who did *not* fuck up five years ago.

SIX

Michael

SEVEN YEARS AGO

"**MS. COLLINS,** IF YOU could approach for cross..."

The girl in the second row stands at our professor's moderation. Her heels thump-clack on the thin carpet. My gaze starts at her shoes, then trails up her pencil skirt and over her oxford, tucked in at her narrow waist. Did she actually dress up for debate class? My eyes linger a moment too long on the buttons open at her chest. Her cleavage is hollow, her breasts small, which is why she can get away with her shirt dipping low and still look professional. Her back to the class, she winks when she catches me eying her.

A tremor shivers under the skin of my fingers. I pull in a slow breath and clutch the podium. There's nothing to be nervous about. This is a gen-ed class. These kids are here to get their communication credits and move on. But this is what I do. This is what I work my ass off for. This girl probably just did a Google search of death penalty pros and cons, but I've been studying political science for almost three years. I knew whichever side my professor assigned me—kill 'em swiftly or let 'em rot—I'd persuade the class. My opening speech in support of the death penalty was solid, and I'm versed enough in the subject that there's nothing anyone here can throw at me that I can't handle. Especially not mediocre cleavage.

She's standing beside me, facing the class, so I can't keep unbuttoning her shirt in my mind.

"Mr. Bishop," she starts, "to clarify from your speech, the majority of inmates on death row are murder convicts, correct?"

"Yes, that's correct."

She steps toward the class with her hands clasped behind her back. "Murder is a tricky crime to convict someone of, don't you think? Sure, we can know beyond a reasonable doubt who committed the crime. But can we really ever know what goes on inside the head of a killer? That's where everything gets slippery, doesn't it? *Motivation.*"

Her jaw cuts over her shoulder to look back at me, but she leans her hands on the table in front of her, the table with no students sitting at it. "You, of course, understand the line between first- and second-degree murder in California is the defendant's intention, determined by the prosecutor—is he a cold-hearted killer, or did he just snap?"

"Right."

"Murder One, an offense punishable up to death, and Murder Two, an offense punishable up to life." She lets out a sigh and pivots to look at me head-on. "Mr. Bishop, have any of your loved ones been convicted of murder?"

What? "No."

She walks my way with that same confident sway of her hips as she continues. "Six years ago, twelve people who had never spoken to my father convicted him of Murder Two instead of justifiable homicide. I mean," she opens her hands in front of her, then folds them at her waist, "there was no doubt he killed my mother. I watched him do it."

Holy fuck.

"But what good father wouldn't attack the person who was raping his daughter with a hairbrush? Is it his fault his momentary rage gave him more strength than he realized? Is it his fault her skull cracked against the toilet when he threw her out of reach of his little girl?"

It's quiet for easily five seconds before I realize she's waiting for me to answer her question. "I—I wasn't there. I'm not sure."

"The jury was sure. And speaking of intentions, could any of those jury members have been swayed by the fact that he was a six-foot-two,

two-hundred-pound black man, and his victim was a petite white woman?"

All the moisture in my throat disappears. "Perhaps."

There's no time for me to respond before she continues. "Think about it. Has there ever been a time in history when we could trust that we knew the motivation of a killer or the motivations of those killing him? And even if we did, who is to say those motivations are justified? Our culture? Our politicians? Our law enforcement? Have we forgotten the Holocaust, or the lynchings of African Americans not one-hundred years ago? What about those in Darfur who are slain *today* because their president legalized their slaughter? Really, how could it ever be just for a civilized government to *order* a person to take the life of another?"

Her eyes, dark as coal, burn into mine. I have no response. How the hell do I have no response?

"We're all human," she adds softly. "None of us can ever be sure if we have enough justice on our side to kill one of our own." She nods to Professor Brown. "No further questions."

My head dips low between my locked elbows. What the fuck just happened?

"You can take your seat now, Mr. Bishop."

I glower up at him. He's smirking. Ass.

It's safe to say my team lost the debate. Ms. Collins's little stunt—and it was a stunt—

changed the opinions of four of our classmates, which sounds like a mild victory, but it's not. It's monumental. She transformed four people's convictions. And I didn't change one. If this had been a courtroom, she would have owned the jury.

I find her eating lunch on the lawn an hour later, an hour that I used to research the validity of her story. She's dressed down now, in a UCLA hoodie and jeans that flaunt the curve of her hips.

Towering over her, I ask, "Senior poli-sci major?"

Her eyes scroll up to mine, the bite of apple she's chewing tucked in her cheek. Her slim neck rolls as she swallows her food. "Freshman, English."

I pinch my eyes, then murmur, "Fuck me."

"No, thank you."

"That was a dick move."

"What was?"

"You made up that story about your dad."

"I did?"

"There is no prisoner in California convicted for second-degree murder with the last name Collins."

She shrugs and takes another bite of her apple.

"You cheated."

"How?"

"And your argument wasn't even solid."

47

Her face lights up with a smile that raises her eyebrows. "I know. I played you *so hard*."

"You didn't play me. You lied!"

"Not that it's any of your business, but Collins isn't my father's last name."

"What *is* his last name?"

"Let me get this straight. I just publicly relived one of the darkest moments of my life, all to entreat my peers to contemplate an issue I hold deep convictions about, and you are not only fact-checking me, but calling me a liar?"

I drop to sit on the grass in front of her so we're eye-to-eye, but she's still sitting higher than me because of the slope. Feels appropriate. "I think I owe you an apology."

"Just one?"

I smile and offer my hand. "Michael Bishop. Pedantic asshole slash aspiring law student."

She draws a reluctant breath and slips her hand in mine. "Dillon Collins. Aspiring to graduate and get a job."

"I'm sorry," I whisper. "No kid should have to go through that."

Her hand retreats, and her eyes return to the lunch in her lap.

It's one of those moments where I know exactly what I *should* do, but I figure today's already a loss so I might as well do the opposite. "You're in the wrong major."

"Wow, you're on a roll."

I list on my fingers, "You're a brilliant debater, you have a personal investment in the justice system, you're fucking intimidating, you're eloquent—"

Her eyes are snarky when they slash to mine. "You're shocked that I'm so articulate?"

I bite by bottom lip, but a snicker sneaks through. "Not at all." She watches me as she continues to eat. "English is fine. It's great. But you should look into law school. Maybe take some philosophy or government classes, study for the LSAT next year. I—I could help you if you want."

She tilts her head and studies me a moment. The scrutiny of her gaze is unnerving. "I'll think about it, Michael Bishop." She tips her chin up, motioning for me to stand. I do, and, when I sling my bookbag over my shoulder, she adds, "See you in debate."

I nod. "Maybe I'll win next time."

Her right cheek tightens with a crooked smile. "Unlikely."

SEVEN

Cal

Estlyn is dead asleep, flat on her stomach next to me. Her lips are puckered open, and there's a circle of drool on her pillow. The sheets are only halfway up her back, the dawn light casting a soft shadow in the valley of her spine. She looks exactly the same as she did yesterday, which is why it's so hard to leave. But she did say *meaningless* and *no strings attached*. Waking up next to her felt meaningful, so I stepped out before any strings could be attached.

Like yesterday, I tug the covers up to her shoulders, careful not to wake her before I climb out of bed. I dress in the bathroom and gargle with some mouthwash I find under the sink. Her mouth is closed and her face out of her spit puddle when I return. I lean over her nightstand to leave a note on the legal pad—which apparently lawyers, like writers, have scattered all over their homes. On it, I jot down another E. E. Cummings quote:

"(lady i will touch you with my mind.) Touch you, that is all, lightly and you utterly will become with infinite care the poem which i do not write." Be back with breakfast soon.
—Linus

"If you're coming back, you need the key," she mumbles, her eyes still closed. "If not," she raises her middle finger high in the air, then drops it into the pillow beside her.

Laughing, I brush the hair away from her face. "I was going to pick up breakfast. Anything you want?"

Rolling over onto her back, she stretches her arms above her head. "Something with bacon and eggs," she says on a sigh. "There's a café on the bottom floor and cash in my wallet."

"You paid for dinner last night. I got breakfast."

She shakes her head. "Gino paid. I just left a tip."

"Gino?"

"The owner. He's a friend." She looks me up and down. "Hey, you promised to fuck me."

"You were up till four. I didn't want to wake you."

"Oh, speaking of which"—she rolls over and grabs her phone—"a friend of mine is an agent at WME. I texted her last night about taking a look at your work, if that's okay."

Holy shit. William Morris Endeavor is one of

the biggest talent agencies in Hollywood. Who the hell is this girl?

She skims her texts and adds, "Whatever agent you have now, you should fire. I don't handle writer's contracts, but from what I can tell, yours was dogshit." She pauses as she reads the screen. "She says she will."

"Wow, that'd be amazing. Thank you." I don't have an agent. I didn't need one since my dad got me the job on his show right out of college. I don't tell her that, though, because it'll make me sound like one of those spoiled Hollywood brats who can't get work without Daddy making a call. I don't tell her because then she'll figure out my dad was the one my girlfriend left me for. I don't tell her that he fired me because he said that Erin was a better actress than I was a writer and he didn't trust me to write her part. And *of course* he had me sign a dogshit contract.

"Do you mind sending me some samples of your work and some kind of cover letter for me to pass on to her?"

"Of course, I'll do that this morning. Estlyn, thank you. Seriously. I mean, I love Elliot, but I can't live *and* work with him. He's driving me insane. I've just stopped responding when he talks to me, because he never stops."

She exhales a breathy laugh. "Well, I like having you around," she shrugs, "if you ever need to crash here."

Ha! *Meaningless sex* my ass. She likes me back. When I reply with a silent smirk, her forehead wrinkles with regret. "That sounded too relationship-y, didn't it? Let's rewind. Did I say I liked having *you* around? I meant I liked having *your dick* around."

I laugh. "Thank God. For a second I thought you wanted me for more than just my body."

"No! That'd be so inappropriate." Her smile is soft and sheepish, not confident and intimidating like usual. I lean in to kiss her, then make up for not being inside her when she woke up.

EIGHT

Estlyn

I USE A GOOGLE number when I call targets.
Now, this means they don't usually pick up the
first call. Once in a solar eclipse do they listen
to a voicemail I leave. But everyone checks their
texts.

*Mr. Calloway, I'm Zoe Whitaker, an attorney
from After Twelve. I understand Mia Sanchez is
suing you for wrongful termination. If you want
her to drop the suit, call me at this number.*

I send the text when Linus is out grabbing
breakfast, then hop in the shower with my cell's
ringer on. Shampoo is running over my eyelids
when it rings. I finish rinsing as fast as I can and
lean out of the shower to answer. "After Twelve."

"It's positive!"

Oh. Rory. "Oh my God! Congrats! Tell Liv—"
My phone beeps. "Hey, I'm getting another call."
I swipe over to the restricted number. "After
Twelve."

"Miss Whitaker?" Someone's desperate. And

why did he block his number? I just texted him.

I reach back into the shower and tighten the faucet until the water turns off. "This is she."

"This is Ron. You texted me about Mia Sanchez."

"I did. I wanted to discuss alternative ways to settle your dispute over her termination from *When We Fall*."

"A mediation?"

"Not exactly. She is happy to drop the lawsuit if you agree to a few terms."

He groans. "Terms? I prefer the half-assed lawsuit."

"Which is why you called me back within ten minutes of my reaching out." There's a long pause, but I know he's still there when his sigh statics the speaker. "You understand that she isn't suing your producer or network, she's suing *you*, personally, for three million dollars."

"She won't win."

"Maybe not. But those damn lawyers will cost you a nut and a half, won't they? And from what I've heard, your finances are rather precarious. Your ex-wives take over sixty-five percent of your paycheck in alimony. Then, of course, there's the house you recently refinanced to keep from going bankrupt, but now it's underwater, isn't it? And you were late on your last mortgage payment. But sure, what are a three-million-dollar settlement and some legal fees to an acclaimed Hollywood director such as yourself?"

Now comes the moment when the scale tips. He takes a breath—a strangled inhale, then an acquiescing exhale. "What will it take to drop the suit?"

"She has two terms. One, fire Taylor East."

He scoffs, but I press on.

"Two, make a public apology to Mia Sanchez and, in fact, all the women in the industry for tolerating East's behavior. I recommend using the 'Time's Up' hashtag if you use Twitter."

"I can't fire my lead actor in the middle of shooting a season."

"Not even for producing and distributing child pornography?"

"He was acquitted."

"So was O.J. Look, the producers of *House of Cards* had no problem firing Kevin Spacey when he admitted to sexual misconduct. Ridley Scott even reshot *All the Money in the World* to cut Spacey out. I'm afraid you have no excuses, Mr. Calloway."

"You don't understand what that would cost the show. You're not thinking about the writers, the cast, the crew. This move won't be easy to justify to my producers. I'll lose my job."

"I disagree. You're doing the right thing. You'll be hailed as a hero of feminism, of the movement for protecting women in the industry. Alternatively, you could go broke fighting to protect a kiddie-porn producer."

My apartment door opens. Linus is already back.

I lower my voice. "You have twenty-four hours to comply to these terms. After that, I'm afraid, the consequences will only intensify."

"Are you threat—"

I hang up, then turn the shower back on. "Had to take a call," I shout over the sound of the water. "Be out in a sec."

"No worries!"

After I get out of the shower a few minutes later, I slap on a bra and panties. My wet curls hang around my shoulders as I hug Linus from behind in the kitchen. I press my cheek into his white, V-neck tee. The scent of him softens me until my eyes involuntarily close and my hands trail up to his chest. Good. I need to like him. Or at least appear to. "Thanks for breakfast." I squeeze him tighter, then let go. "Wanna eat on the balcony?"

"There's only one chair."

I slip on his button-up shirt as I head toward the sliding-glass door. "I've sat on your lap before, Linus."

I curl against his chest in the chair as I piece apart the sandwich he got me. It's still overcast, like it is most mornings on the beach, and just cool enough to justify snuggling against him. I swallow a piece of bacon and say, "Rory knocked up his wife."

"Hey! That's great!" He sips his coffee. "Do you already have nieces or nephews?"

"No. He's my only sibling, and this is their first."

He nods, his expression full of questions I haven't answered.

"I'm aware we don't look related."

His chest deflates with a nervous laugh. "Are you guys half-siblings or—"

"Adopted."

"Which one of you? Sorry, is that too personal?"

I shake my head. We're not even near personal. "We both got placed in the same foster home. It was emergency care, so they were supposed to keep us for a week, tops. But, you know how the foster system is."

"I don't, actually." Right. Beverly Hills born and bred.

"Well, a week turned into a month, and a month into six. By that point, we weren't really an emergency placement anymore, so they would have had to uproot us again, which agencies don't like to do. Besides, they were having a tough time finding me a home since foster parents get to choose the race and age of the kids they take. I was already twelve, and I think people were afraid that I was going to be violent." Please. Even then, I was too smart to hurt anyone physically. "Not to mention, Rory was an Orange County kid, and they're hard to place because the standards are so damn high for the homes. The kids get more of a say than in the other counties, and Rory pitched a fit anytime his social worker talked about taking him away from me. So, the Collinses were stuck with their emergency placements. They ended up adopting both of us when I was sixteen."

I haven't looked up since I started my explanation, but I feel him staring down at me. "How old were you when you went into foster care?"

"Eleven."

"Where are your parents now?"

Ooh... Now we've hit personal. I shake my head and then rest it on his shoulder. "In hell."

LINUS LEFT ME A few minutes ago with a kiss on my cheek but no phone number. I like it. He has my work email and my apartment address. I know where he works. I'll have his email and old home address once he sends me his writing samples.

Oh, and I have all his emergency contacts.

I find a well-worn contact in my phone and tap it. After a few rings, Dean answers.

"It's before nine. This better be worth it."

"You know, people with real jobs wake up before nine on Thursdays."

His sleepy voice perks up. "Why are you

acting so happy?"

"I'm not happy. Icy sludge pumps through my veins like always."

"Bitch, don't lie to me."

"Once again, it's not okay for you to call me a bitch."

"Holy God, you met a boy."

"A *boy*? What are we, still in college, drinking light beer from cans like impoverished Valley girls?"

"Ooh… there is a boy. Praise the Lord, the drought is over!"

"I have a story for you."

"Yes! Tell me everything. What's his name? How'd you meet? Did you sleep with him? You did, didn't you? Sweet Jesus, someone needed to clear the cobwebs out down there. Five years is too—"

"It's not a story about him."

"So there *is* a boy!"

"It's about Ron Calloway, the director."

"Really? I wouldn't think he was your type. You're not usually into old—"

"The story, Dean. The story is about Calloway. I'm not seeing him."

He huffs in melodramatic disappointment. "Yeah, yeah. Story. What is it?"

"Okay, are you aware Calloway hired Erin Kennedy to act in the third season of *When We Fall*?"

"Erin who?"

"Yeah, exactly. Calloway knew that Kennedy was struggling to break into the industry for six years and offered her the part in exchange for sex."

"That's not a story. That's a Tuesday in Hollywood."

"I know it's not all that sordid in and of itself, but if you can get her on record saying that he coerced or—"

"—Threatened to make or break her career based on her response to his advances, then we have a lead."

"Right. I have her number, and I can round up a list of other young actresses whose careers he's made if you need comparable stories."

"I'll let you know."

"And remember, he just fired Mia Sanchez for the scandal she had with Taylor East even though he was the perv in the situation. I have her contact info, too, if you need it. But you *have* to reach out to Erin this morning and let me know what she says."

"*Morning*?"

"Yes, Dean. It's that time of day adults get out of bed and start working."

"Fine," he whines.

"If the lead pans out, I need you to write the story, but you can't show it to your editor."

"How long will I have to wait?"

"Until Calloway's twenty-four hours are up."

NINE

Cal

"SO, DINNER WENT WELL?" Elliot crosses his arms and leans his hips back against the bar.

My jaw is starting to cramp from forcing myself not to respond, but I have no interest in talking to him about Estlyn. He formed an opinion about Erin after their first meeting and never wavered from it. And it wasn't a good one—which he never failed to remind me of when I caught her cheating on me with my furry-assed dad. For now, I'm enjoying the luxury of not having a relationship for him to comment on.

"She seems a little… out of your league."

Thanks, man.

"Intimidating. I mean, it's hot as fuck, don't get me wrong, but what the hell is she doing with you?"

He's goading me. I'm not going to fall for it.

"What does she do for a living?"

I step away from him to wipe the counter before the rush-hour crowd makes it sticky again.

"What's the sex like? Is she—"

"God," I groan, "shut up."

"Shit," he whispers and pushes me into the back. "The she-devil is here."

"What?" I turn around to see Erin, teary-eyed with half her makeup wiped away, her skin pink and blotchy. She always hated this place. What is she doing here?

"Want me to—"

I put my hand on his shoulder and say, "I got it," as I make my way to her. She wipes her eyes with her thumbs when she sees me. I press my hands on the counter and barely glance at her. Her blonde hair is up in a messy bun. She's not all pretty and perfect like she usually is. Good. It'd be even better if she could see who I woke up with this morning.

My stomach twists, and it feels like my sternum cracks when her blue eyes meet mine. I'm still not past the *I'm so disgusted by you that I want to throw up when I see your face* stage. I'm also lingering in the *I miss you every minute, how could you have betrayed me?* phase. Erin was my first real girlfriend, not counting the handful of girls I got to second base with in high school. (*Remember second base?*) That one-night stand with Estlyn was wholly outside my character… which is probably why it is no longer a one-night stand.

I avert my eyes from hers when I ask, "What

can I get for you?"

"Cal," she sighs. I hate how she says my name, like I'm something to deal with, like every word I say will be the wrong one.

"If you're not going to drink, give the seat to someone who will."

She glares at me. "Shot of tequila."

I slam the glass on the table, fill it, then pass it to her.

She throws it back, then rests it on the bar. "I think I fucked up, Cal."

"You catch on fast."

She shakes her head with a soft, defeated laugh. "God, just listen for once."

"I heard everything. You and my dad fuck very loudly."

"Why do you think, Cal?"

"Because you're a manipulative, selfish, would-eat-her-own-young bit—"

"Oh, cut the adjectives. You're a better writer than that."

"That's nine dollars," I say as I turn to help someone else. She can pay Elliot. Or not pay at all. I don't care as long as she gets the fuck out of here.

"There's a story that's going to break tomorrow about your dad and me. TMZ has it for now, but others will get it."

"Another Fat Tire?" I ask the guy next to her. The customer nods, so I get to work—work being opening a bottle of Fat Tire.

Because she never knows when to shut up, Erin keeps talking, "Read it. Please. I'm not asking for a second chance—"

I hand the guy his beer, then cut my eyes to Erin. "Good, because I'm fresh out of those."

"But maybe you'll understand why I did it."

I roll my eyes, then move down the bar. A few minutes pass before I return Erin's direction. All that's left in her place are two five-dollar bills and her empty shot glass.

TEN

Estlyn

I HAVE A GOOGLE alert set for *Taylor East*, *Ron Calloway*, and *Mia Sanchez*. The only pings I get are a picture of East shirtless on the beach with some fifteen-year-old, bikini-clad singer. I look forward to that sex tape coming out. Not like that. God. I just mean the DA is more likely to get a conviction the second time around.

It's been just over twenty-four hours, and the word *fired* has yet to come up next to East's name. I text Calloway.

I'm disappointed we could not work together to give Ms. Sanchez the justice she deserves. Enjoy the TMZ headline with your name in it.

I pick up the phone to call Dean. He texted me after his interview with Erin Kennedy yesterday. It went just as I had hoped. Whether or not Ron abused his position of power to fuck Erin, Dean had given her the opportunity to tell a sob story, and Erin liked that narrative better than the one that would've followed the headline, *Cheating*

Girlfriend Bangs Her Way to Fleeting Fame. Besides, no one would read that.

After four rings, Dean answers. "Bitch, it's not even eight. Be a millennial. Text!"

"I need you to run the Calloway story."

"Okay, let me text my editor *like a normal person.* Hang on." He must be tapping on his phone because he doesn't talk for a few seconds. "You owe me."

"You called me bitch. Again. We're even."

"No, I meant you owe me details about this boy."

"Ugh. I'm going out to State today," I huff, "but meet me for drinks tonight."

"Yay! Don't get shanked."

"How would I ever get shanked?"

"If you make it back alive—"

"I will."

"There's a club downtown I want to take you to."

"No. We're going to this bar in Culver City."

"Why?" he whines. "You never go along with any of my suggestions."

"Because one, I'm more likely to get shanked at whatever club you take me to than at prison today, and two, *the boy* will be at this bar."

"Ooh!"

"Post the story, Dean."

"Love you, bitch."

"Love you more, dumbass." I grab my

messenger bag and flip my car keys around my finger a minute before forcing myself to stand from the couch. I make this drive all the time. There's nothing to be afraid of. Lightning can't strike the same place twice, right? Except that I'm pretty sure that happens all the time.

ELEVEN

Linus

ELLIOT SLAPS HIS PHONE on the bathroom counter. "She-devil is a trending topic."

I spit my toothpaste in the sink and glance at the screen. In bold, black type are the words, *Ron Calloway Accused of Sexual Misconduct*. Beneath the headline is a grainy picture of him getting coffee alone. He's unkempt and scruffy in it—the shitty slob of a dad I remember. I rinse the remaining minty foam from my mouth, then pick it up to read.

Amid When We Fall's recent child pornography scandal come new allegations of sexual misconduct. Thursday, Erin Kennedy (24) came forward with accusations that director Ron Calloway (61) made sexual advances toward the actress during her audition for his hit Netflix series.

"Ron asked the casting director to leave when I walked in," Erin told TMZ. "He handed me a script for a different scene than the one I had rehearsed. I

skimmed the page and realized it was a sex scene…
Ron put my hand on his c**k and told me to read
the first line."

The story is interrupted by Erin's headshot,
the pretty and perfect face I knew—a stark
contrast to the one I saw yesterday.

"I know now I could have said 'no.' But at the
time, it all happened so fast that I didn't even think
about the option of not doing what he told me."

Kennedy went on to say she felt too "ashamed"
and "disgusted" with herself to tell anyone. "Then
I got the part. I was so desperate for work, for
money to cover rent, that I didn't consider turning
it down. After what happened next, I wish to God
I would have."

She reported that Calloway "hounded"
Kennedy for sex incessantly, reminding her of her
"expendability."

This allegation is the most recent to rock the
series When We Fall, coming just on the heels of star
Taylor East's trial for production and distribution
of child pornography after he released a sex tape of
himself and underage costar Mia Sanchez, whom
Calloway is rumored to have fired after the scandal
broke.

"He has a habit of treating his actresses as
dispensable," an anonymous When We Fall cast
member commented. "It was as if he was punishing

Sanchez for whistle-blowing instead of holding East accountable. It sent a real message, you know? 'Let them f**k you or find a job somewhere else.'"

Kennedy shared this actor's fear for their job security. "I know that I likely won't have my role when this hits the web tomorrow," Kennedy added, "but no job is worth this."

TMZ reached out to Calloway for comment. He declined.

There's a pang in my ribs—guilt stabbing the inside of my chest—as the last couple of months come into focus. Erin's distance. Her insecurity. Her drinking more than she ate. But it was hard to think clearly about any of that when I couldn't get the image of my dad on top of her out of my head.

The betrayal hadn't cut the deepest. It was the realization that the woman sleeping next to me wasn't the person I thought I'd known.

In the five years we dated, I never saw Erin flirting with my dad or anyone else. I wasn't a jealous boyfriend, or maybe I was just blind, so I never worried about her screwing around. But I did see Dad's endless parade of too-young-for-him actresses leaving his house when I lived there. A handful of those faces are familiar to more than just us now. If they haven't been on his show, they've been on others.

How many of them are going to come forward

now?

How many will it take to ruin him?

It's noon. I have about an hour before I have to be at the Dive to open. I slide my wallet in my back pocket and grab my keys. My hand is on the doorknob when Elliot speaks up.

"Load of bullshit, right?"

I hand him his phone back. "I don't know."

"Well, whatever. It doesn't matter if it's the truth. She didn't have to keep fucking him. After that first time, she could have said no."

I exhale to relieve the shame in my chest, but it doesn't help. "Maybe."

"You're not going to go see her, are you?" When I ignore him to slip on my shoes, he raises his voice. "Cal, she sought out that reporter. She volunteered the information. If she wanted to work things out with you, she would have gone to you, not *TMZ*."

I'm not going because I expect an explanation. I don't want to work things out with her. I don't need to find out the truth or exchange forgiveness. I'm going because she's likely scared shitless right now, and I don't know who else she has.

I don't offer Elliot a second glance before I duck out the door.

TWELVE

Estlyn

LANCASTER IS THE WORST city in California. It's ugly and brown and the main attraction is the state prison. Also, it's twenty-five degrees hotter here than at my place. But I make the hour-and-a-half drive out here twice a month to see my favorite client.

I'm such a familiar face here now that the correctional officers are almost kind when they wand and search me. Probably because my client is a model prisoner. Probably because he doesn't belong here.

As usual, the officer leads me down the long hall until we reach the visitors' area, a bare, fluorescent-lit room with just one window to let in the sun. It always smells in here, smells like harsh cleaners and stale air and men—that's the most overwhelming odor. I get a glimpse of my client through the windows set in the walls. He's already seated at a table in his prison-issued orange. Even seated, his broad shoulders boast how massive he is. A few grey hairs are swirling in the black now. He's starting to grow old in here.

He stands when he sees me, his eyes bright and gentle. His arms reach out, and the guards pretend they don't see when I drown in his embrace. He kisses the top of my head before he releases me. I look up into the eyes that match mine. "How you doin', baby girl?"

"I'm doing good." Always *doing good*. For all he needs to know, I've been *doing good* for the last fourteen years. Because he can't stand being stuck in here, helpless, if I'm doing otherwise.

I know the guilt he shoulders is overwhelming. Three missed graduations. One daughter legally orphaned. Two strangers adopting her as their own. My last name isn't his anymore. It kills him, but he understands. He knows I'm not ashamed of him, only afraid for him. He still worries about me constantly, still thinks of me as the little girl who was abused, still bears remorse for not being there to stop it. I immediately regretted telling him what Brock did to me. There's nothing more unravelling than watching a bulky inmate weeping thunderstorm-size tears. So, I don't tell him things anymore.

"How are you?"

He shrugs. "Doing fine."

I open my bag and pull out three novels for him. "I thought you might like this series. The guy at the bookstore told me it is up-market if not literary fiction." My dad was a high school English teacher in his past life. I love listening to him tear apart *literature these days*. Though, it makes it hard to find books that can wow him. "Oh, and they don't have it in your library yet, so just donate them when you're done if you don't want them."

"Thank you."

"Also…" I pull my dad's file. "I *finally* found a judge who is going to try to get you early parole even after—"

"Dil—" He puts his hand on mine.

"Hayes," a correction officer warns. Dad lifts his hand.

"We talked about this. You're not working my case."

Oh, did I mention my favorite client is the most fucking difficult one in the world? "I know we talked," I continue as I sift through the papers in front of me, "but kids never listen to their parents."

"Please. This isn't your problem to solve. After last time—"

"The judge is Christina Reyes. She's progressive and ruthless and older than God himself, so we need to take advantage of her offer before she retires or, more likely, dies."

"Sweetheart." His tone is gruff and commanding, the way it gets when he's about to put his foot down. "No. I'll call my lawyer. He will handle it."

My eyes sting as they raise to his. "No. He'll fuck it up. We have one shot at this, and I'm the one who is going to take it."

"This burden is never something I'm going to allow you to bear, so stop picking it up."

The tear slides down my cheek until it drops from my jaw. "Are you kidding me? Do you know how hard it was for me to get this meeting with Reyes?"

"I'm sorry, but you know—"

"No, I don't know, Dad. I don't know what the hell your problem is with me trying to get you out. You bitch all the time about missing my life, but you won't let me do anything to make you a part of it." I jab my finger at him. "You *owe* me this. You owe me a chance to have a dad."

He's calm as he watches me cool off from my tantrum. "Are you finished?"

I roll my eyes and nod.

"I'm trying to be your dad. Dads don't ask their daughters to sacrifice for them. It's supposed to be the other way around. You went through it twice; I'm not doing this to you again." His eyes dart back and forth between the dark circles under mine. "You're tired, baby girl."

"I'm never tired."

"Well, stop smoking so much crack."

I breathe a laugh. "It's just a shit-ton of Adderall. Don't worry."

He smiles but stiffens his resolve. "Give the case to my lawyer. If I find out that you were involved beyond that, I won't let him meet with Reyes. Understood?"

I sigh. "I don't understand, but sure."

"Put all that stuff away. I want to talk about your non-work life."

"What non-work life?

His lips curve in a half-smirk. "Are you spending time with any men who are not gay and not Rory?"

I squint at him. "Have you met any women lately who aren't COs and not your daughter?"

"I already did the marriage thing."

I respond with a caustic, "And the end result makes me want to sprint down the aisle."

"Sweetheart, it's been five years."

I dig through my bag again. "And I have up to ten according to this pamphlet I had Dean print out for you." I slap the fabricated psychological information on the table in front of him.

He laughs as he reads, "'Estlyn is an accomplished lawyer and doesn't need a husband to have a fulfilling life. Also, her eggs will be good for at least fifteen more years. That being said, if you have further concern, I have volunteered several times to fertilize said eggs because I think we'd have a beautiful ethnic swirl of a gayby.'" He looks at me. "I never said anything about your eggs."

I rub my chin. "Yeah, Dean's biological clock is ticking. But the point is, I have some perfectly good sperm up for grabs, so you don't need to worry about me meeting a guy."

"Sperm isn't going to look after you or marry you."

"That's an interesting challenge."

"Dillon—"

"Why do you think I need someone to take care of me?"

He leans in and lowers his voice. "How are your nightmares?"

"I don't have them anymore."

"Don't you lie to me, sweetie."

My eyes sink to my fingers fidgeting on the table.

"Why aren't you sleeping?"

"I never sleep."

"Yeah, but you're sleeping less."

How does he always know everything? He's not even around! I can't look at him when I whisper, "He's coming after me."

"He's out?"

I nod.

"Shit." He runs his hands down his face. "He knows it was you?"

I shake my head. "Not yet."

"Okay. It's not that bad. You're a smart girl. He's not going to find you. But *this*," his finger stabs the table, "is why you need someone—"

"Who, Dad?" I snap. "Who am I supposed to have? Or tell? God," I rub my temples, "I shouldn't even have told you. You worry about everything."

"Sweetie, please don't worry about me."

"What about Michael's family? What if he goes after them? And if I'm exposed, then Ror is, too. Dad, he's having a kid."

"Dil, they're not going to get hurt."

I bury my face in my hands. "The one time I was sloppy, I dragged him into it."

"You weren't sloppy. You were devastated. And indignant."

"And involved. That was the problem. You can't see clearly when there's still blood in your eyes."

"Just..." he breathes, "try not to be alone, alright? Stay at a friend's or even Rory's when you can. Don't drive yourself anywhere. Call a car."

"You know I hardly drive anymore."

"Good. My lawyer will get me out of here, alright? You just take care of yourself until I can."

I wipe a racing tear from my cheek. "Just hurry, okay?"

THIRTEEN

Michael

"On the board is the schedule for the winter quarter. As you can see, our next tournament is in only two weeks…"

I turn my attention from our debate club president to the door at the back of the classroom. It clicks shut before Dillon sneaks into an available seat. She's hiding in her thick, wavy hair and fitted leather jacket, apparently unsure if she should be here. I smile and nod her way, but it only makes her slouch and twist her fingers on the table. Is she actually wanting for confidence? Did something happen to her between the end of fall quarter and now? I didn't know she could operate at a level lower than hubris.

I move from my chair at the front and hunch over on my way to the empty seat beside Dillon. I lean to her ear and whisper, "Debate team?"

She turns so our faces our inches apart. "I figured it'd be easy since you would fact-check everything for me."

My eyes trail to her bottom lip, pink and full and coated with the slightest sheen. I am *not* imagining sucking it. My eyes snap back to hers. "Are you still an English major?"

She nods. "Are you still a pedantic asshole?"

I pinch my lips with my teeth to keep from laughing, then nod.

"Can you, uh"—she glances at the board, then back at me—"Do you have time to talk after this?"

Hell yes. "A little, yeah."

"Thanks," she whispers before straightening up in her chair.

It's almost midnight when we grab coffee on campus. She leads me to a semi-secluded table and plops her bag there. Her dark eyes spark with intensity when she looks up at me. "You have an internship with a defense attorney, right?"

How does she know that? "I do. Why?"

She sighs. "Okay, you remember my dad?"

"Of course."

"Okay, well, about four months ago, the California Supreme Court granted him a retrial."

"Wow! That's incredible. That almost never happens."

She doesn't look excited. Why isn't she excited? "Michael, his lawyer is shit. This is his only shot, and she's going to fuck it up."

"How do you know?"

81

"She's a public defender because Dad won't let me pay for him to have a decent lawyer." Before I can refrain from asking how the hell an orphaned college student has enough money for a lawyer, she adds, "So, she hasn't even met with him—"

"And when she does it will be for fifteen minutes, if that."

She sighs. "Right. The scary thing is that there isn't DNA or some lost witness that can exonerate him. His actions aren't on trial; his character is."

"Is he the protective father who rescued his daughter, or is he a violent black man who lost it and smashed his wife's head against the toilet?"

She nods, then whispers, "What do I do?"

"God, Dillon. I don't know." When her eyes sink to her coffee, my gut plummets with the weight of her hopelessness. Shit, does she know I can't stand seeing her like this? Is that why she came to me? "...But I can see if my boss is available to meet with you or your dad. I'm not sure if your dad will accept that, but we can try."

Her eyes brighten, and I feel a little lighter. "Really?"

"Yeah." I cross my arms and shrug. "Of course."

"Thanks. I have the money. I swear—"

"No problem." I sip my coffee, then snicker. "Stalker."

She rolls her eyes. "How'd you get such a good internship? Aren't those hard to come by?"

I try not to wince when I answer, "My uncle is a partner."

She smirks, then bites the bottom lip I'm still *not* fantasizing sucking.

"You knew that."

"Bishop and Colburn Law Associates. Figured you were related somehow."

"Damn."

She reaches across the table, takes my phone, and texts herself my number. "Maybe you should adjust your privacy settings on Facebook." Her phone buzzes with her text as she returns my phone.

"Maybe." When she stands to leave, I sputter, "Will I see you at debate?"

"Nah, I'll have to deal with enough of that shit in court over the next couple years."

"Makes sense. You're still not interested in law school?"

She shakes her head. "I'm sick of the law."

"Then go to school so you can change it."

A smile plays on her lips. "I underestimated you."

"Yeah?"

"You might actually be good at this whole persuasion thing. Maybe try it on a girl sometime."

I *am* trying.

"Night, Mike." She waves as she turns away.

I shut my eyes and sigh. "Night."

FOURTEEN

Linus

IT'S A STRANGE FEELING knocking on the door I once lived behind. There aren't any paparazzi here, which isn't surprising. Erin isn't famous. My dad is. They are probably swarming my dad's front lawn, the lawn of the house he can no longer afford. We love watching the great collapse, but we'd rather not see what becomes of those in their wreckage.

Erin answers the door with her phone to her ear. Seeing her is like getting hit with two trains speeding opposite directions—one hits me with guilt for being blind to her pain and pushes me to hold and comfort her forever, while the other slams into me with rage and jealousy. Because at the end of the day, she chose to betray me for months. That first encounter wasn't her fault. What my dad did was shitty and misogynistic and an egregious exploitation of his power. But all the others were her choosing her career over our relationship. Not to mention the ick factor, irrespective of overgrown asshair. I'm not ready to understand that yet.

"I gotta call you back," she says, then hangs up without waiting for a response. "What are you doing here?"

Uh… What am I doing here again? After the weirdest pause I could create, I ask, "Are you okay?"

She hugs herself and leans against the doorframe. "No."

"Is it true? What you said in the article?"

"I told you it would be."

I nod while I figure out what to say next. "I'm sorry."

Erin's sharp blue eyes slice up to me. "But…"

I groan into my hands. "God, why didn't you tell me? I mean, I get that you were ashamed or whatever, but it's *me*. We could have gotten through this if you had just told me the truth. You didn't have to let me move out. You didn't have to shit on five years of our lives."

Her eyes close, and she takes a deep, slow breath. "You're right."

I'm *right*? Really? This is the first time I've been right in five years. I'm not sure I like it. Because Erin won't look at me. Maybe she's waiting for more, waiting for me to yell again about how she hurt me, how she let me hurt her when I never intended to. But I'm not sure I have anything else to say. And I'm not sure if she has anyone else right now. "Can I, uh…" I take a measured step toward her. "Can I hug you?"

Erin snickers. "Sure." I pull her to my chest and hold her as long as she'll let me. It's been only a month, but I've already forgotten how perfectly she fits me. The top of her head hits just below my chin. I nuzzle my cheek against her hair to smell the sweet scent of her shampoo. She's slender enough for me to wrap my arms around her until my fingertips graze the opposite sides of her waist with ease. She relaxes into me, and my chest aches. I hate her and I miss her and I never want to see her again. And I love her. That's what pisses me off most.

She gives me more time than I expected. Half a minute passes before she lets go.

"Did you lose your job?" I ask.

"I don't know yet." She sniffs and wipes under her eyes with the back of her fingers. "I wasn't due on set today, and I'm not exactly speaking to Ron. I'm sure I'm fired, though."

"Let me know what happens, okay?"

She nods.

"I gotta go to work, but…" I squeeze her shoulder before I walk away, "hang in there."

I'm halfway to my car when she yells, "Cal?"

I spin around. "Yeah?"

"Are you still fresh out of…" She shakes her head. "You know what, I'll text you when I find out about work."

"I might have one. I don't know yet."

Her lips curve with the slightest hope. "Thanks."

I nod before climbing into the driver's seat.

FIFTEEN

Estlyn

My NERVES KICK UP as the Uber turns onto Bentley. This was a bad idea. That article came out today about Linus's dad and ex-girlfriend. And I'm about to drop in on Linus at his place of work with the writer of that article in tow.

I turn to Dean. "Hey, so maybe don't mention what you do for a living tonight."

"Why? People love talking about my job."

I'm sure they do. "You know the *boy*?"

"The one we're stalking at the bar?"

I roll my eyes. "Well, that article you wrote about Ron Calloway…" I cringe and look out my window.

"Yes…"

I'm still watching the cars pass when I say, "Linus is sort of related to him."

"How related?"

"His son."

"His what?"

"Linus is Ron's son."

"Jesus."

"And Erin Kennedy is his ex."

Dean rubs his temples. "You're taking your murder weapon back to the crime scene. Honey, the police are there!"

"I know. It's bad. But I—"

"We're going somewhere else." He grabs the back of the passenger seat and pulls himself forward. "Excuse me. My friend has made a terrible error in judgment. We can no longer go to our destination. Would you be able to take us to—"

I put my hand on Dean's arm. "It's fine. We're fine," I call to the driver. "Just don't talk about your job, okay?"

"Can I still go by Dean, or should I come up with an alias like you?"

I flip him off.

"You're buying drinks."

"Don't pretend you ever do."

"Why are we doing this? Can't we just do your stupid game, then go back to your place, drink wine, and think up names for our gayby?"

"My dad doesn't approve. Said your sperm doesn't equal a husband."

"Well that's just offensive."

"I agree."

"When did you find out Ron and Linus were related?"

Damn it! I thought we'd moved on from that.

I clear my throat. "My cases are confid—"

He lowers his voice to a whisper. "You fucked him for his contacts!"

"I didn't even have the case when I—"

"You said you didn't want to sleep with anyone after Michael because no one would ever be *Michael*. That he was the love of your life, and you'd never date anyone again. That your heart wasn't broken but crushed, the pieces scattered, never to be mended, blah, blah, blah."

I glare at him. "Your sensitivity is heartwarming."

"Then you hook up with a guy for a *case*? It's like I don't even know you!"

He looks out his window but holds one finger out at me, wagging it—not his hand, just his finger—back and forth.

"As I was saying, we hooked up the night before I got the case. Then we hooked up again the night after I got it."

"The second time was for the case?"

I rest my head against my window to avoid his gaze.

"What was the first time for?"

What am I supposed to say? *I was scared to sleep alone with Monroe out of prison, so I whored myself out to feel a little safer?*

"Alright, Est, you got the information you needed. You took down Ron Calloway."

"We don't know that yet."

"What the hell are we doing here?"

The Uber stops at the curb. "We're getting a drink."

He pushes his face so far into my personal space that my eyes nearly cross trying to look at him. No one has ever stared at me so intently. It's creepy and awkward, and I hate it. "What are you doing?"

"Trying to decide if you are bonkers horny and making up for a five-year dry spell, or…"

"Ahem," the driver clears his throat.

I open the door and step my stiletto heel onto the sidewalk, adjusting my backless silver dress as I stand. Dean climbs out behind me. He shuts the door, then brushes the front tuft of his dark hair with one finger, using the car window as a mirror. The Uber drives away in the middle of his grooming.

"Does my hair look okay?"

"Dean, it looks exactly the same all the time." He doesn't stop adjusting his shirt buttons, his collar, his pockets, everything—even when we're at the door. "Why are you so fidgety?"

"I'm excited to meet the first guy to ever compete with Michael."

Asshole. No one competes with Michael.

SIXTEEN

Michael

SIX YEARS AGO

"**HOW OLD WERE YOU** when your father first abused you?"

God, I hate this prosecutor. It's been a year since Uncle Will took over Dillon's dad's case. Today is Dillon's turn to testify for the prosecution. She's been sick for weeks over it.

My uncle stands. "Objection. Lead—"

"He never abused me," Dillon interrupts.

The prosecutor doesn't wait for the judge, but instead clicks the monitor remote, displaying a doctor's note. "Do you remember this trip to the school nurse's office on April 3, 2001?" She reads, "'Dillon requested a sanitary napkin. I asked if she was on her period, though she is too young to have one. She was confused and asked again because she was worried that the blood would soak through her pants. I asked why she was bleeding. She refused to answer.'" The prosecutor clicks her heels against the wood floor on her way back to the stand. "Miss Collins, do you remember this?"

"My mom usually sent me to school with pads after she raped me, but she must have forgotten that time."

"She forgot? Or was she out of town?"

"I don't remember."

"Your mom had a conference in Dallas from April second through the fifth. How could she have raped you? Isn't it possible that your father caused the injuries that brought you to the nurse's office that day?"

"No. You can bleed days after you are—"

The prosecutor talks over Dillon. "Is it possible that your dad was the one who raped you all that time?"

"No."

"Is it possible that your mom was too intimidated by your father to report him and instead covered for him?"

"No, he would never—"

"Is it true that when she threatened to report him, he bashed her head in against the toilet?"

"No!"

The attorney swanks to her table and holds up an evidence bag containing a hairbrush. Dillon's childhood blood is still crusted on the bristles. My stomach twists. That's her blood. That's the weapon her mom used to assault her as a child. I never disbelieved her story. Neither the prosecution nor the defense questions that someone abused Dillon with it, either. But seeing it makes it real. Because I can't see that scabbed hairbrush without seeing the child who endured it. And now the prosecution is putting her on trial.

"Then why are your father's prints on your hairbrush?"

"Because he did my hair, bitch."

Oh, shit. *Don't lose it, Dil.*

The prosecutor swivels to the jury, smug and satisfied when she clicks a picture of the Hayes family on the screen. "This photograph was taken four months before your mother's murder."

Will stands and shouts, "Objection!"

Murder. See? she's the worst.

"Withdrawn. You were ten in this photograph, correct?"

"Yes," Dillon answers.

"And at this time, you're the same height as your mother. About the same weight, same build, would you agree?"

"Yes."

"Was this before or after your mom was diagnosed with lupus?"

"I'm not sure."

"This was about a month after your mother was diagnosed with a devastating illness, an illness that can affect every part of the body—her brain, her heart, her lungs, her kidneys, her joints. A month after she found out that her immune system had declared war against her body."

Dillon shrugs, waiting for a question.

"You want us to believe that your mother, suffering from a crippling autoimmune disease, physically subdued and raped you when you were the same size as she and far healthier?"

"It wasn't *crippling*. It was mild. And if you think that children fight their abusive parents off once they're physically an equal match, you're an idiot. You don't think the Menendez brothers could have kept their mother from molesting them as teenagers? Of course they could have. It's not about strength. It's about power."

Oh, boy. *Rein it in.*

"Answer my question, Miss Collins. Was your mother physically capable of raping you?"

"Yes," Dillon hisses, "because she did."

"But was your father stronger than she?"

"Yes."

"So, physically, was he *more* capable of raping you?"

"If you want to reduce him to his physicality— which, by the way, Americans have been doing to black men since they brought us over in the hulls of ships—"

Oh, Dillon. Your soapbox will still be there after court is dismissed.

"—then, yes, I suppose he was more capable. If you want to treat him as an actual human with a soul and a conscience, then no, he was

95

incapable of raping me because he isn't a rapist."

"You were placed in foster care after your father's arrest, right?"

Dillon catches her breath before answering, "Yes."

"Did you want to go home, to live with your father?"

"Every day."

"Did you know that it is common for children who are removed from their homes to crave their parents, even those who are abusive?"

"Sure."

"Were you so desperate to be home that you lied to the court about the circumstances surrounding your mother's death?"

She scoffs. "Of course not."

"Did your father threaten to kill you like he killed your mother if you admitted that he was the one who raped you and murdered your mother?"

"No!"

The prosecutor, calm as ever, nods and steps back toward the jury. "Was your father aware that your mother was abusing you?"

"Not until he saw it, no."

"How do you know?"

"Because he would have stopped it."

"Was this the first time your father used physical force against your mother?"

"Yes."

The prosecutor crosses her arms and cocks her head to the side. "Can you be sure? Were you with them all the time, even before your birth?"

Dillon's eyes close as she draws an agitated breath. "No."

"Was your father aware of your mother's health condition?"

"Of course."

"Do you know the symptoms of lupus?"

"I know *her* symptoms."

"And what were they?"

"She was tired a lot. And achy."

The prosecutor throws the next exhibit onto the monitor. It's a medical report. "The lupus attacked her lungs, causing inflammation. So not only was she tired and weak, she struggled to get enough air to breathe. Is that right?"

"Sometimes she had trouble breathing," Dillon relents.

The prosecutor clicks her fake nails on the jury bar and asks, "Even though your mother was in this fragile, indefensible state, your father felt the need to assault her to protect you? Couldn't he have used as little as half the force he did to remove her from you?"

"Do you have children?" she snaps. By that blazing look in Dillon's eyes, I can tell she's stringing together a chain of expletives in her head. I can also tell that she's on the verge of being declared a hostile witness.

"Answer the question, Miss Collins," the judge admonishes.

Dillon is undeterred, restraining herself to her seat but inching toward the precipice of it. "If you saw your child being brutally raped, would your focus be on how to have a civil negotiation with the rapist, or would it be on keeping her from jamming a hairbrush into the kid's vagina again?"

"Miss Collins," the judge continues, voice raised, "answer the question, or I will hold you in contempt."

"You know what he did as soon as he threw her off me? He picked me up asked me if I was okay. He rocked and soothed me as I cried. He dialed 9-1-1 to get an ambulance for each of us. It wasn't that he was intent on killing my mom. He was intent on protecting me."

"Miss Collins," the judge repeats.

Answer the damn question, Dil!

"Yes, he could have used less force," she responds coolly to the prosecutor.

"Miss Collins, do you want your father to be released from prison?"

"Yes."

"Why?"

"Because he's innocent."

"Do you think you're impartial? You are his daughter, after all."

"No, but it doesn't mean I'm wrong."

"If he did intend to kill your mother, do you think he should be absolved because he did so in your defense?"

"I—" Her eyes flinch to her dad, then to me. She's asking us a question neither of us can answer. "I don't know enough about the law to say if he should be."

The prosecutor lifts her shoulders in one of those fake shrugs litigators do. "If I killed my child's rapist, would that be just?"

"Depends on the circumstance."

"What kind of circumstance would justify my killing this rapist?"

Dillon tilts her head back and forth. "Well—"

Oh, God. She's not thinking. She knows exactly what she's going to say, and it's going to put her in a jail cell.

"—I suppose if the rapist were a black man like my father, you wouldn't even be indicted."

"Miss *Collins*," the attorney chastises, but it doesn't dissuade Dillon, whose hands are in the air, preacher style.

Don't do it, Dil.

"Really, though. Would we be here if my mom had killed my father to keep him from raping me? No! She'd be a heroine. She'd—"

"Miss Collins," the judge shouts, "this is your last chance."

Dillon forces a breath through her nose as she quiets, and the prosecutor closes in.

"You said I'd be justified in killing my child's rapist if the circumstances warranted it. According to the law, you're correct. However, we're relying on you, an admittedly partial witness, to convey those circumstances?"

Dillon grits her teeth and answers, "Yes."

"Just to be clear, we know your dad killed your mom, right?"

"Yes."

"Was she too weak to defend herself against him?"

She sighs. "I guess so."

"And you want your father out of prison?"

"Yes."

"So," she weighs in one hand, "we have the facts that point to murder, and," she raises the other hand, "we have your biased opinion that suggests justifiable homicide." She turns to the jury and asks, "Shouldn't we convict based on facts?"

"Objection!" Uncle Will calls out. "Leading the witness."

"Withdrawn. No further questions."

I TAKE A FINAL, shaky breath before I knock on Dillon's dorm-room door.

Muffled from within she shouts, "Fuck off!"

"It's Michael." Why am I so confident that it's not me she wants to fuck off?

The door clicks as she opens it. Her hair is up in a disheveled pony, a thick headband covering the curls at her scalp already undoing her hard work of straightening them. She pretends she wasn't just crying, but is terrible at it. Her makeup is worn off, her cheeks and eyes puffy.

"I brought you a present."

She sniffs. "Yeah?"

After I open the ice-packed lunch box, I pull out a Diddy Riese ice cream sandwich. "I had them make it the gross way you like—peanut butter cookies and strawberry ice cream."

A sigh splinters a reluctant smile across her face. She swings open the door, then waves her arm to usher me inside.

"I could have just made you a peanut butter and jelly, then stuck it in the freezer," I say as I hand it to her. "It would taste the same."

"Not even close." Dillon unwraps it before handing it to me. "Try it."

I take a bite of the melting ice cream and chilled cookie. It's almost as disgusting as I thought it would be. "Nope," I say with my mouth full.

She hops up onto her bed and I follow, our backs against the wall that meets the long edge of her twin mattress. Her tone is matter-of-fact when she says, "So, my dad's going back to prison for life, and it's all my fault."

I shift to face her. "What are you talking

about? You did incredible today."

She shakes her head, swishing silent tears down her cheeks. "No, I fucked his whole case up, Michael."

I've never been so alarmed by tears before. This is the first time I've seen her cry. There's something that feels catastrophic when people as strong as her break, like the earth beneath them might crack, too. "Are you kidding? Did you see how scared she was? She had to try so many lines of questioning—"

"And I still said what she wanted the jury to hear."

"Dil, that's not your fault. They haven't even gotten a chance to lay out the defense yet. It always looks bad when you have to hear the prosecution day after day. Soon, everyone will hear his side. It'll get better. I promise."

She huffs and leans her head on my shoulder. "Okay."

I'm hesitant when I wrap my arm around her. It's hard to tell what the boundaries are with a friend like her—a friend I have an irremediable crush on. I've wanted to ask her out since debate class, but I haven't figured out a good way to do it since she's been so preoccupied with the trial. It seems insensitive to say, *Hey, when you're not worried sick about your dad's fate or preparing to testify about how your mother molested you right before your dad killed her—oh, or studying—*

would you like to go out? Needless to say, after a year of bonding over the commonality of my uncle being her father's defense attorney, I have been sufficiently friend-zoned.

I'm surprised when I feel the warmth of her cheek against my chest. Dillon's not usually one to need any kind of care, or, if she is, she doesn't come to me for it. This is the least intimidating she's ever been. It's throwing me off balance. Does she want me to... *comfort* her? That's what a normal girl would want, but this is Dillon. There is no manual for how to interact with her.

She's so quiet as she cries that I don't even notice she started again until I feel her tears soaking through my T-shirt. Her ice cream is hardly touched, so I take it from her hand and set it on the wrapper on her desk. I pull her body into mine as her bawling grows audible. She curls up against me, slipping her legs over mine so that she shivers in a huddle against my chest. Her fists ball up my shirt as she lets out a sob.

I press my lips into her head and breathe in the fragrance of her hair. "I'm here, Dil. It's okay," I whisper.

Her voice shudders when she asks, "Have you had sex before?"

Um... what? What does this have to do with anything? "Yeah, why?"

"Voluntarily?"

I nod.

"What's that like?"

Oh, God. She's not just crying because she feels the burden of her dad's trial. She's crying because she has to relive being raped over and over for it.

And she doesn't know anything different.

"Um, it's... vulnerable, I guess. And sometimes awkward, or it is the first time. The first time is pretty much a guaranteed disaster." She laugh-sobs, then snuggles closer against me. "And, if you love the person, it's still... perfect."

"Did you love them? The girls you slept with?"

"There was only one, and yeah, I did."

"Why aren't you still together."

I shrug. "Sometimes things just fall apart."

She scoffs. "That's a cop-out."

"Her parents didn't approve."

"Ah."

"Then we left for different colleges. She tried to make it about that, but she got distant well before then."

Her voice is steady for the first time when she says, "I'm sorry."

I hug her tighter, my cheek against the top of her head. "Don't be. Now I get to be here with you." She pulls away, poring over my face with her gaze. Ah! Shit! I shouldn't have said that. "I mean, not that— Not in a romantic—"

I can't finish my sentence because her lips are parting mine. I'm *finally* getting to suck her bottom lip, and *holy shit* it is way better than I thought it would be. It's full and soft and she tastes like peanut butter cookie, which is now the hottest taste ever. I could be deathly allergic to peanuts and I'd still kiss her like that moron in *Romeo and Juliet* who kisses the poison from her dead lover's lips. *That's the way to die, Jules.*

Dillon's hands grasp at my shirt until they're beneath it, until they find the waist of my jeans and tug me on top of her. We're tangled together a minute before my conscience kicks in. We can't do this. She's a mess and just trying to cope. This isn't fair to her. Even if she doesn't realize it now, I know she'll regret this tomorrow.

I force myself to pull my face from hers. "Dil, what are you doing?"

Her expression falls in an instant. I watch her eyes squeeze shut, and her breath releases like I've just punched her in the nuts. "You should go."

I don't move. "Why?"

She shoves at my chest, trying to push me off her. I don't budge. It's cute how frightening she is all the time, but how harmless she seems right now. A little worrisome, actually. Girl should do some pushups. "If you didn't want me, you could have said something, asshole. You didn't have to lead me on for months."

I stroke her cheek with my thumb, then let my fingers explore the soft skin of her neck. My face stoops so my lips can follow the trail my fingertips blazed. "You have no idea how much I want you."

"Then what's your problem? Let's have sex."

I press off the mattress so I'm hovering over her again. "What?" I say with a nervous laugh. "No."

"No? Why not?"

"Because this isn't going to be some rip-the-Band-Aid-off thing where you're numb and don't care who you have sex with as long as it's your choice."

"I *do* care, idiot! I want it to be you!"

"Oh." I stretch my neck back, so I can see if there's truth to her words. "You like me?"

She throws her hands in the air, then lets them slap against the bed. "Yes! For, like, a year. I was waiting for you to make a move, but you never did."

I bury my face in the warmth of her neck and groan. "We could have started dating a year ago?"

I feel her chest shake as she laughs. "Apparently."

My hand curves first her ribs, then her waist against me.

Her breath is hot in my ear when she asks, "Are you really going to make me wait any longer?"

SEVENTEEN

Cal

I'D SAY I HAVE a realistic perception of myself. In the looks department, I'm safely a seven. I'm only 5'10", but I'm on the leaner side of 160 pounds—in shape, but not broad-shouldered, thick-necked ripped. If I worked out more, I might squeak up to a 7.5. I don't tan without freckling, which brings me down a point or two, but Erin used to tell me I had a jaw and cheekbones that would make Gisele envious—not sure how I feel about that compliment still—and eyes like sea glass, so I think that earns me some points above five.

The guy holding Estlyn's hand is a solid ten. He's the classic tall, dark, and handsome type that girls think about when they're having sex with sevens like me. I don't know anything about designers, but I'm fairly sure the clothes he's wearing are more expensive than my entire wardrobe. And he probably pays more than ten dollars for his haircut. Rich and hot. Just like Estlyn.

I'm a seven. He's a ten. She's a ten. Math fucks me every time.

Shit, maybe I *am* the jealous type. Or maybe I'm just like this with Estlyn. Maybe it's her short, silver dress and the fact that I can't stop wondering if she's wearing panties or not. She didn't wear panties under her dress when she took me to dinner the other day. I found out in the bathroom when I reached up her dress to pull them down and felt nothing but her warm skin.

I should be relieved that Estlyn is with someone, right? It's confirmation that she's unattainable. Erin loves me. And I still love—

My God, is Estlyn wearing panties or not? She's bending to sit, and there's no line on either ass cheek. A thong maybe? Nothing? Agh! I gotta know.

Nope. Doesn't matter. As I was saying, Estlyn is with someone, and Erin and I love each other. Sure, she fucked my father, but we can move past that, right? Couples work through infidelity all the time. This means I might not have to sleep on Elliot's couch much longer.

Estlyn and Mr. Ten kick back at a narrow booth. She tosses her ebony hair behind her shoulder and huddles over the table to him. I've never seen her hair straight before. It's like silk falling down her back.

Shit! Mr. Ten catches me staring. My eyes go on a frantic search for something to busy myself with. A middle-aged man in scrubs brandishes his empty glass at the other end of the bar. I make my way toward him, but another bartender beats me there.

"Excuse me," a guy calls out from behind me. I turn to see Mr. Ten pressing one hand into the bar.

I will myself to be polite, but I can't force a smile. "What can I get for you?"

"Two mojitos, please."

Before I can bite my tongue, I ask, "Are you sure one of those shouldn't be a wet gin martini, stirred? Or an Old Fashioned?"

His mouth curls, Grinch-style, into the widest grin I've ever seen. "Estlyn ordered a martini, but she pissed me off on the way here, so she's getting a disgusting drink *and* she's paying for it."

I chuckle both with relief and because this guy is the most instantly likable human I've met. He's a ten in looks, but also a six on the Kinsey Scale. I set a martini glass on the counter.

"Don't do it." Mr. Ten/Six is glowering at me when I look up at him. "You would give her a mojito, too, if you knew what she did."

I put the martini glass away and clank two highball glasses against the bar. "What did she do?"

"She's hiding something from"—he places his hand over his chest—"her best friend slash aspiring gayby daddy."

"Gayby daddy?"

He flicks his fingers down, dismissing my question. "Oh, it'll never happen. Her dad won't give his blessing, and she doesn't do anything without his blessing. Which is a shame, because can you imagine how gorgeous our blatino child would be?"

"I thought her dad was dead." I'm not sure why I just blurted that out.

"Why would you think that?"

Oh, maybe he's talking about her adoptive father. I shake my head and ask, "How do you know she's hiding something from you?"

"Also," he adds, pointing a finger at me, "I'm pissed on your behalf because she's using you for more than just sex."

I spit, flabbergasted, but I don't have a drink in my mouth, so I just kind of mist saliva everywhere until I cover with a laugh. "What?" Does that mean she likes me?

He rests his elbow on the bar and leans across it to me. "She's not as tough as she seems. Go easy on her, okay?"

What the hell does that mean? Is that supposed to answer my question? I nod as if I understand.

"Dean, by the way." He reaches his hand out to shake mine.

"Cal," I say as I shake the hand of the most instantly likable and impossible to converse with person I've met. I hand him the drinks I hopefully didn't spit in.

"Nice to meet you," he calls over his shoulder as he walks away.

I pour a couple of draft beers for some other customers before I hear, "Linus!" behind me. Turning, I find Estlyn glowering and ushering me over with her finger. I approach, then lean over the bar so I can feel her breath on my lips as she scolds me.

"A mojito? Am I nineteen?"

"Jury's still out on that one." I glance past her at Dean, who winks at me. Ordered the wrong drink because he was mad or because she was too chicken to come over here herself? "Show me your real ID, and maybe I'll make you the drink you ordered."

She rolls her eyes and opens her clutch. She's about to hand her license to me, then presses it face down against the bare skin of her chest. "Can you keep a secret?"

"Of course."

Estlyn slaps the ID on the bar, picture-side up. I pick it up and slide my finger over the picture that must be from high school. The license is about to expire. She is twenty-five, but her name isn't Estlyn E. Collins. It's Dillon D. Hayes. "Besides my birth certificate, that's the only thing that still has my birth name. I couldn't bring myself to change it after the Collins family adopted me."

"D?"

She huffs out a reluctant, "Destiny."

I don't notice right away that I'm smiling like an idiot at her confession. It feels like I'm winning whatever game we're playing. And she's adorable when she's losing. "Dillon Destiny Hayes. That's beautiful."

"Sure," she says as she snatches it out of my hands. "Martini, please."

I nod and get to work. "Why don't you go by Dillon anymore?"

"I shouldn't even go by Collins anymore, but it's on my diploma so I keep it in case clients want to check my qualifications."

"Oh, yeah? What firm do you work for?"

She pauses as if she's deciding how much truth to tell me, if any at all. "Show me you can keep a secret, and maybe I'll tell you."

I ditch the cocktail shaker on the counter and whisper in her hair, "Which mob do you work for?"

She throws her head back and laughs. "I don't work for a mafia."

"A gang?"

"No, it's far less exciting than that. I simply handle sensitive cases and, for my safety, prefer to keep my personal and professional lives from overlapping."

My gut knots a little. "Are you in danger?"

Her dark eyes harden like marble. For a

second, they splinter, giving me a glimpse of the tumult behind them. Then she blinks and bites her lip. "Aw, you worried about me?"

"Should I be?" I pull back and pour her drink. The olives plunk against the glass before I slide it her way.

"What are you doing after your shift?" she asks before sliding an olive off the toothpick with her teeth.

"I'm gonna troll bars for a hot bartender to have a longer-than-one-night-stand with."

"Look no further." She points behind me. I turn to see Elliot, and my chest shudders with laugher. "Mission accomplished. I'll see you at ten."

Before she steps away, I reach across the bar for her wrist and tug her back. I catch her cheek in my hand and kiss her. When my lips taste hers, I realize I never had this with Erin—this overwhelming clash of emotions, this feeling of being held under by a crashing wave and not knowing when I'll come up for air. I was never this thrilled with her. Or this nervous around her.

Or this afraid for her.

EIGHTEEN

Estlyn

"**YOU HAVE ONE HOUR,**" Dean repeats as we step out of the elevator and onto the top floor of the Ritz Carlton. "That's the longest I can be compelled to carry on a conversation with bland bartender Brooklyn."

"I might need a little more than that."

"No, you lose your edge at an hour. You cash in at nine-thirty, okay?"

"Oh, relax. You know it's my last one."

"You always say that."

"Nope, I'm burning this bridge to the ground." Hopefully I make it to the other side before I catch on fire, too.

I open my clutch for the guard at the door to examine its contents. He takes my coat and Dean's, then pushes the heavy white-and-gold door open for us. As we do every week, Dean takes a seat at the bar to drink his weight in complimentary cocktails, and I drop ten grand in cash on the runner's table to get my chips.

There are three open seats at the game table. I take the one with another available next to it.

It's Texas Hold'em. He's had a shitty week. This is how he blows off steam. He'll be here.

He better be.

I'm up four grand when Taylor East finally grants us the privilege of his presence. I make a show of re-crossing my legs and pat, then caress, the open seat next to me. He takes the bait even though I'm closer to his age than he'd prefer. Maybe Linus is right. Maybe I do look nineteen. Taylor's hand slides down my exposed knee after he sits in the seat I lured him to.

We play two hands like this, his hand playing my thigh like the neck of a violin, begging me to taste his ear as I whisper, "Where's that good girl tonight?"

He turns to face me, but I don't lend him my ear. I let him whiff the subtle scent of alcohol on my lips, let him think I'm tipsy enough to open my legs. "She's not so good, you know." His lips curl into a smirk as he sits up. "Call," he says and throws a few chips into the pot.

"Raise a thousand," I reply, my eyes on his as I toss in my bet. My gaze with Taylor's doesn't break until it's his turn to, hopefully, fold. I'm not confident I hold the cards to beat him *and* that asshole investment banker two seats over.

But Taylor doesn't fold. Neither does the asshole.

The dealer flips the river. Taylor and I both check the table to find the fate of our hands. The two pair I had didn't turn into a full house. It's just a two pair. There aren't even any faces in it. I turn back to Taylor and bite my lip to keep from smirking.

"Check," he says, repeating the asshole's bet.

"Baby, that's no fun." My gaze leaves his just long enough to collect my chips. I toss them and meet his eyes. "A thousand."

The third player slides his cards toward the pot. Fold.

And then there were two.

"What's it going to be, babe?" I lean in and giggle, "Should I take your money now, or do you want to gimme a little more?"

"I always wanna give you a little more."

I can hear Dean rolling his eyes from the bar, that's how ridiculous this is.

Taylor throws in a few more chips. "Five hundred."

"Live a little." I drop my chips onto the pile one by one so he can hear each of them clink with the others. "Two thousand."

His tongue rolls over his bottom lip as he studies me, like he's considering his position for the first time this game. I control my breath and simper as if I enjoy being the object of his speculation. He's fifteen-hundred dollars away from finding out if I'm playing him.

I beg him to let me play him. "Aren't you curious?" I wink.

"Don't you wish I was?" Taylor throws his cards in the center, surrendering the pot to me.

Before I scoop up my earnings, I slither my hand up his leg. "*I'm* curious. Is she really as filthy as you say she is?"

I release his thigh to collect my money, but he snags my wrist. "Fuck, yeah."

I shrug him off, uninterested. "I won't believe it until I see it."

"Then let me show you."

Jackpot. I tip my head toward the glass door behind us, and Taylor nods.

I cash in while I'm on top and meet him on the narrow balcony. His back is slouched against the railing in that effortless, Instagram-ready style he's rehearsed so much it's become habit. My fingers dance over the phone cupped in his hands until my middle one flicks the edge of it from his grasp. I turn so he can pull my ass against his groin and grope my waist and hips while I flip through the child-porn pictures of his new girlfriend. These are all selfies she took naked in the mirror with pursed or parted lips and fuck-me eyes. In other words, nothing that would incriminate him. Finally, I swipe to a blurry, flesh-colored image with a play symbol over it.

I spin around so we're junk-to-junk, so my hands are behind his head, so he can't see the screen. My lips purr against his ear as I rhythmically grind against him. "God," I breathe, "I love watching you fuck." His fingers dig into my ass when he pulls me as close as we can get with our clothes between us. One of his hands is so focused on getting up my dress that he doesn't even notice that I've sent this video and three others to my email. His finger is on its way inside my thong when I drop his phone over the ledge.

"Shit!" I yell and wrench away from him. My hands grip the railing as I watch it somersault to the pavement below. Taylor isn't fazed. His hands are grasping at the inside of my thigh, tugging my legs apart and back around him. I giggle as his phone meets its ruin with a soundless splat. My arms slip back around his neck. "Sorry, where were we?"

"Est!" Dean shouts from behind me. Good, he wasn't too deep in vodka to hear my signal. "Our car's here."

I tug Taylor's earlobe between my teeth and let him shiver when I say, "Next time, invite me."

Both of my palms thrust off his chest as I pivot to strut to Dean. He takes my hand and loops it through his arm. At the hall door, the guard drapes my coat over my shoulders and Dean's over his available arm as we leave with twice the money that I had when we arrived.

We both keep our mouths shut until we're in the back of the Uber. "Incorrigible idiot," I mutter to Dean.

He smiles half up his cheek. "They always think they are untouchable when they get away with it once."

"I'll tip you once we're back at my place."

Dean kisses my cheek. "Thanks, bitch."

I rest my head against the window as we turn left through a traffic light. Seconds after, red and blue lights flash behind us. There's a whoop of a siren. My heart hits the brakes, then the accelerator. Then the brakes again. Start. Stop. Start. Stop. Threatening to flatline as we veer into the nearest parking lot.

I should be thinking about my clutch stuffed with twenty grand in cash or the phone full of child porn I haven't yet turned over to the police. But all I can see is Michael.

Our driver rolls down his window to the greeting, "License and registration." Those three words are how it starts. How it always starts.

I study our driver. By his accent and olive skin, it's clear he was not born here. He hands over the ID and registration he'd already retrieved from the glove compartment. "Was I speeding or something?"

The officer glances over the documents with his flashlight. "No, but did you know your left brake light is busted?"

I want to shut my eyes. I want to squeeze Dean's hand. I want to puke. But I can't do anything that would make me look suspicious. One wrong move is all it takes to turn this from a broken brake light into a barrage of blood and bullets.

The driver rubs his face. "No, I didn't."

I can't breathe when the officer shines his light over my window. But then it continues to the trunk, then back to the paper in his hand.

"Can you put your foot on the brake?"

I assume our driver complies.

"Yeah, it's actually shattered if you want to take a look. Maybe you got hit in a parking lot or something."

"Shit. Are you serious?"

"Yeah, they musta got the light bulb, too, because it's not lighting up. I'll be right back," the cop adds as he taps his hand on the roof of the car.

Dean is silent as he covers my hand in his. He's not afraid, but he knows I am. When the officer returns with his printed warning, my vision clouds with purple and black spots. I'm not sure the last time I breathed. When I try to take in air, my lungs refuse to expand. The inside of the car darkens as my breaths pulse—shallow and desperate. I press my hand to my chest as my heart protests beating against the pressure inside my ribs.

Through the thick grey, a light shines into my face. Then, the license-and-registration voice addresses me.

"Miss, are you okay?"

The door beside me swings open, and I slump over and vomit out of it. The officer crouches to support my sweating shoulders. That's when I glimpse the gun on his belt. I ease my hands to the back of my head. "Please," I repeat as I hyperventilate. "Please," *gasp*, "please," *wheeze,* "don't."

There's this sudden cacophony around me—Dean's panic, the driver's concern over the possibility I puked in his car, and the officer radioing for an ambulance. Then, the lights shut off.

NINETEEN

Michael

Six Years Ago

God, what is she doing to me? I don't lift my face from her pillow when I answer, "Yeah, we should probably wait." Dillon's hands return to the waist of my jeans and slip between them and my boxers.

Come on, Dil, help a guy do the right thing.

"Why?" she breathes as she pops the button of my jeans loose. "What's going to change between now and whenever you think I'm ready?"

I shut my eyes as if that's the same as shutting out the slender fingers teasing my dick. "I—I don't know. Maybe you could get counseling?"

Her chest arches into me as she cackles. "You really think I'm going to keep talking about what happened?"

"You should."

"Michael, nothing is going to change."

It takes every ounce of willpower in my body to roll off her and onto my back. My hands cover my eyes and muffle my groan. "I don't want to

122

hurt you."

The sincerity returns to her voice. "Then show me it doesn't have to hurt."

My eyes meet hers—naked and honest. This is the first moment that I see she isn't manipulating me to get her way. She actually does want something different, something better. And she wants it from me.

"Okay." I ease the hem of her shirt up her waist, my fingers grazing her skin as I do. They stop when I reach the wire of her bra. "You *have* to tell me if you change your mind. It doesn't matter when—"

Her throat rises when she swallows. "I won't."

Dillon lets me kiss every inch of her body as I undress her. Beneath her clothing is a breathtaking fragility—delicate but strong, like glass—glass that will shatter in the wrong hands.

She's trusting my hands to hold her.

Her anxiety surges as her body responds to me. Hard between her legs, I feel her swollen and wet, but her hands are unsteady as they trace my body. They're shaking and scared.

I rest my lips against her ear. "It's okay if you changed your mind."

"I didn't."

"I'm going to get a condom, okay?" She nods as I reach to my wallet on the desk. Her eyes tighten shut as I roll on the condom. I brush my fingers back through the hair she freed from her ponytail minutes ago. "Dil, take a breath and relax."

A tear slips down her temple. "What if I can't feel anything? Or if it hurts? What if I'm too fucked up down there to—"

"Hey," I whisper before taking her bottom lip between mine. "Then we'll figure it out. We have plenty of time."

She nods, taking the calming breath I asked her to. A shuddering inhale passes her lips as I enter her—the kind that makes me know she can feel me. And it doesn't hurt. As if that wasn't the best sound she could make, she lets out a laugh. It's so breathy and short that it's barely a laugh, but she does. I press up onto my hands so I can see her face. "What?"

"I'm not completely fucked up." I wonder if that's why she's waited until she was nineteen to do this—because she was afraid she was ruined and didn't want to find out for sure.

Cupping her cheek in my hand, I kiss her as deeply as I'm buried inside her. We take every movement slowly, cautiously. Each sound she makes in response is perfect. I'm in no rush, which is good since it takes a while for her to finally tense and release and melt breathless beneath me. But she does for the first time ever, and she does it with me.

My fingers caress the skin over her spine as she sleeps naked on my chest. My eyes open when I hear something trickling from the desk beside us. I glance over to see a puddle of pink ice cream dripping to the floor.

TWENTY

Cal

IT'S ELEVEN O'CLOCK WHEN I realize I'm an idiot for waiting more than fifteen minutes for Estlyn. She never showed up at the Dive, which is fine. I'm old-man-level exhausted—definitely too tired to go out or have sex. At least, that's what I tell myself as I drop into the front seat of my car. I'm in the parking lot of Elliot's complex when my phone rings. It's not a number I know, but it has a 310-area code, so I answer. "Hello?"

"Hey, is this Linus Calloway?"

"Yeah…"

"Oh, thank God! Jesus, give the girl you're sleeping with your number so I don't have to go through hell trying to get a hold of you!"

"Who is this?"

"Dean. We met at the bar tonight. I'm charming and despicably handsome. Ring a bell?"

And mildly insane. I chuckle. "Yeah, I remember you."

"Okay, so Estlyn did *not* bail on you. She's in

126

the hospital."

"*What?* Why? Is she okay?"

He sighs. "I don't know. They sedated the shit out of her and are running an EKG."

"Holy shit, an EKG? Is something wrong with her heart?"

"Possibly. They're going to do an ultrasound in a few minutes here."

"Does she have some sort of condition?"

"No. I thought she was just having a panic attack or maybe PTSD or something, but they think it's something else."

"PTSD?"

"Yeah. Look, I gotta call her dad before she wakes up and tells me not to. Save this number. It's hers."

"Wait, what hospital is she at?"

"UCLA."

"I'll be there in ten minutes."

TWENTY-ONE

Estlyn

THE PRESSURE IN MY chest has been replaced by a heaviness in my eyelids. But I can still fight them open. I'm lying down inside some room that has a paneled ceiling and lots of beeping and distant voices.

Ah, hospital.

I survived.

My hands inspect my torso and thighs for bandages, but there are none. Instead, they find several wires and adhesive pads stuck to my chest. I push myself upright, but something shoves me back to the bed. Not hands. It was the strength of whatever drug they pumped me full of.

"Dean," I whimper.

Warm skin meets my cheek. "He's on the phone, but he'll be right back."

My head rolls toward the voice. Linus. How is he here? I squint to focus on his face as I sink into his hand. "When did we pick you up?"

His smile is gentle, but his eyes betray

128

something else, something I can't quite figure out. "You didn't."

"Then how did you—" I try to bolt to my feet but flop back to the inclined mattress. "Where's my phone? My clutch?" I drop my legs over the side of the bed, and my body rolls off it with them. Linus's arms and chest break my fall.

"Hey, lie back down."

Dean pushes through the curtain that surrounds the door and taps the screen of my phone. "Hey, look who's awake!"

Linus is propping me up to sitting when I reach my heavy arm out to Dean. "Give me my phone."

He hands it to me. "I already caught you up for the night. You'll just need to heat it up when you get home."

A sigh whooshes from my lungs. That's his code for *I sent the videos to the LAPD tip site. Then I deleted the email account you sent the videos to and from. All you have to do is microwave your phone when you get home to wipe it clean.*

"Thank you," I whisper once I'm steady enough to sit on my own. "Is fifty percent from tonight okay?"

"I already took twenty-five, and I'm not taking any more." He sinks to sit on my bed, then guides my shoulders back to the pillow. "Now lie back down, bitch. You had a fucking heart attack."

I scoff. "I'm twenty-five. I did *not* have a heart

129

attack."

A couple taps on the door precede a young woman in a white lab coat entering my room. "Estlyn?"

"Yep." I raise my hand as if someone else in this tiny room might be the patient.

"I'm Dr. Bianche. How are you feeling?"

"Great." I reach into the gown to rip the sticky pads from my chest. "I'm going to head home now."

"I'm afraid we can't let you go home yet."

Let me? Bitch can't tell me what to do. I watch as she grabs the stool on wheels and takes a seat as she looks through my file. "There's gotta be something I can sign so I can leave."

"Well, let's talk about your condition first so we can make the best decision for you."

My condition. Please. I contain an eye roll as she continues.

"You had a type of heart attack known as a stress cardiomyopathy."

Shit. I *did* have a heart attack.

"The good news is, it's not the traditional type of heart attack, where you have a blocked artery and your cardiac tissue dies. Your heart should return to normal within a couple of months."

"Great. So, I'm okay?"

"Well, no. You still had a heart attack. You have to make some lifestyle changes if you want to keep this from happening again or from having heart failure in the future."

"Lifestyle? I don't understand. I'm not overweight. I don't smoke. I exercise—"

"You're right. You're physically healthy, which is great. But it's called *stress cardiomyopathy* for a reason. I'm talking about changes you can make to reduce emotional strain in your life. Do you have anything causing you anxiety right now?"

I purse my lips and shake my head. "Nothing comes to mind."

"Okay, well it doesn't have to be stressful. It could be grief or anger or even a breakup. A nickname for this condition is broken heart syndrome. Is there anything like that going on right now?"

I feel Dean's eyes boring two holes in my face. "Nope."

The doctor allows me to linger in a silence long enough to show me she's unconvinced. "Okay. We're going to keep you overnight to ensure you're stable before you go home tomorrow. You'll need to take the next four weeks off work. Do you need someone to help you with the disability application?"

I snicker. "I'm a lawyer. I think I can handle some paperwork."

She's unfazed by my insolence. It's fucking annoying. "Do you have a psychiatrist or therapist?"

"No, of course not."

"Okay, we'll send you home with a list of providers covered by your insurance, and I'll set up a psych consultation for you while you're here."

Does she have to say all this bullshit in front of Linus? "Why, exactly?"

"Estlyn, twenty-five-year-olds are not supposed to have heart attacks."

I air quote as I repeat, "Heart attack."

"Estlyn," Dean cuts in, "listen to the damn doctor."

Dr. Bianche holds in a snicker before starting again. "There's only so much I can do for you. A mental health professional can help get to the root of the issue. That way, you won't have such an intense reaction to stress again."

"I can tell you for certain there was nothing stressful about tonight."

Dean clears his throat off to my left. "Nothing? Really?"

Asshole. I grit my teeth just enough for him to hear it. "Nothing."

"He'll just ask you a few questions," the doctor continues. "It's nothing more than that. And do you have someone who can stay home with you at least this week?"

"Sure, of course."

"Oh, yeah?" Dean chimes in. "Who?"

Motherfucker. I didn't invite him to my little heart-attack party. "I have someone."

"Really? What's his name?"

After a super long pause that is probably even longer than I realize because the drugs are slowing me down, Linus answers, "Cal."

Dean's and my heads snap to him. What? He's going to stay with me for a week? Not just stay with me, but take care of me? I just met the guy. Oh, and used the unwitting sap to take down his family. Eh, there was no love lost there.

"And Rory or Dean can hang out when I have to work."

"Linus," I shake my head, "you really don't need to do that."

His rubs his face, cheeks heating with red. Shit, I think I just rejected him. "Yeah, that'd be too much, too soon, huh?"

No. It wouldn't be. I want him around. I'm scared at the thought of being in that apartment alone with my heart on the fritz... *allegedly*. For all I know, my heart's fine. I could have just had some bad fish tacos for lunch. "No, not at all. I just don't want to inconvenience you. That's a lot of pressure to put on someone I've known four days. I'm sure I can—"

"This is her version of begging, Cal," Dean interrupts. "She needs you."

I roll my eyes, and Linus's lips split into a relieved smile.

After the doctor leaves, Linus covers my hand with his and presses a kiss to my cheek. "You okay

133

if I run home and pack real fast?"

"Linus, you don't have to come back here. I can just call you when—"

"Shut up. I want to."

Dean chuckles. "You learn fast."

Linus pats his shoulder on the way out the door. "Thanks for calling, man."

"Yep."

When Linus is safely out of sight, I narrow my glare on Dean. "What the fuck?"

Dean responds with his delicious, evil grin—the *damn it, he's gay* grin—then feigns innocence. "What?"

"You want to talk about returning to the crime scene when the police are there? How am I supposed to work on East's case with Linus in my home?"

"You're not, dumbass. You're not supposed to work at all for a month. You set everything in motion to get Taylor and Ron fired. You might even get Taylor indicted again. You've done your due diligence for your client. Now you wait."

"What about my other clients?"

"Tell them you have to take a medical leave, like a normal person."

"Dean, do you understand how my job works? I don't have paid vacation or sick days. I don't have colleagues who fill in. If I don't handle these cases, I'll lose my reliability. My reputation is my income."

"Or, instead of working, you can tell them you're swamped and they have to wait in line. It'll make you look like you're in even higher demand than you are."

I let out a low growl. "I'll just do what I can from home."

"No. You won't." He throws his hands up and flops back in his chair. "I don't even get why you're still doing this. You have a JD and about a bazillion connections. You could get a job at a firm like a regular lawyer."

"What do you mean 'still doing this?'"

"You gotta drop the vendetta sometime. Your job made sense five years ago when you were mad as hell, but now… you're still trying to right every wrong, and Est," he shakes his head and sighs, "you just can't."

"Maybe not. But I'll right even fewer at some law firm."

Dean scoots his chair up to my bed and takes my hand. This is taking a turn. I don't like it. "Do you really think this is what Michael would want for you?"

My eyes sting. The sides of my throat stick to each other, and my chest aches like muscles after a marathon. No, this isn't what Michael wanted for me. But it's too late for either of us to get that. "You should head home."

"Why?"

"Because you're pissing me off."

"What do you want from your apartment?"

"I didn't mean *my* home."

"Bitch, I'm trying to help you. And do you *really* want to keep all this cash in your hospital room?"

I huff. "Toothbrush, toothpaste, and clothes, please. You know the combination to the safe?"

"Yup."

"And can you wipe my phone while you're there?"

"Obviously. I'll tell the nurse to sedate you again on my way out, so you don't scare Linus away."

I flip him off. He returns the bird as he leaves.

I reach for the remote and turn up the volume on the monitor. The guys were watching *Fresh Prince of Bel Air*. This was my favorite show to watch reruns of when I was a kid. In college, I used to tell Michael he was the Carlton to my Will because I was smooth and sexy in that early nineties kind of way, whereas Michael was... book smart.

He did not appreciate the comparison.

I melt into the pillow and shut my eyes. The beeps of the machines are quiet beneath the sound of studio-audience laughter at Will Smith attempting a pickup line. I never understood why Will tried so hard. He was so pretty.

My lungs inflate against the soreness around them, and I do what I do all the nights I can't sleep—I crawl into bed with Michael. I imagine the weight of his arm over my waist, the curve of my body tucked against his. I pretend to breathe in his scent. I shiver as his lips nuzzle a kiss behind my ear. I hear him tell me to relax, that he's here, and as long as he's here, he'll make sure I'm okay.

He tells me he's not going anywhere.

I'm drifting off when I hear footsteps enter my open door. Must be a nurse. There's no way Dean or Linus is already back. My eyes open to an LAPD uniform.

TWENTY-TWO

Michael

FIVE YEARS AGO

I WOULD BE LYING if I said prison didn't scare the shit out of me. I know that's hypocritical since I work for a defense attorney. And because I hope to work in criminal law after law school. And because the girl I've been dating for a year has her only family here. I know Dillon has been visiting her dad in prison under supervision since she was a kid, and alone since she was eighteen. My palms shouldn't sweat when I walk through the metal detectors or get pat down. But they do.

He's not waiting for me in the visitor's room when I arrive, so I fidget at the table, alone, like I'm relegated to the friendless table in the high school cafeteria. Except instead of a high school, it's prison. And instead of a cafeteria, it's prison. And instead of greasy food, it's just more prison.

It takes Mr. Hayes an hour to arrive. Or maybe two minutes. However long it is, it's not enough time for me to calm down enough to say the words I've rehearsed. But I am relieved not to be alone at the lame kids' table anymore.

I stand the moment Mr. Hayes passes through the door. He reaches his hand out to shake mine. "Michael, right?"

Shit, does he really not remember my name? The shaky smile I manage to offer fades. How am I supposed to do this if he doesn't think I'm significant enough to—

"Nah, I'm just playing, Michael." He releases my hand and gestures for me to take a seat across the table from him. "You're all Dil talks about. What kind of father would I be if I didn't know the guy my daughter was in love with?" We both sit down before he asks, "To what do I owe the pleasure?"

"Well…" As I look up at him, all the words I memorized disappear, and rushed sentences tumble out. "Sir, I want to spend the rest of my life with your daughter. And, look," I put my hands out in defense, "I know we're young, and you and I both know she could do better than me, but she—" I take a ragged breath as I shake my head. "She's the first person I think of in the morning, and each night I want her falling asleep with me until we can't wake up again. I want her to have everything I can give her, sir, even my life if necessary. Do I have your permission to give her that?"

When Mr. Hayes answers, steady and slow, I realize just how frantic my desperate little speech was. "How are you going to provide for her while you're in law school?"

Yes! I was prepared for this question. "It's not ideal. We'll have to live on student loans for a few years, but I have a job lined up when I graduate."

"And where will you live?"

"I've applied for graduate housing. We should have no problem getting an apartment."

He nods. "And when do you plan on marrying her?"

Marrying sounds more real when it comes from his mouth. Half my nerves dissolve into elation. I'm going to marry her. "Probably next summer after she graduates. That way you could walk her down the aisle."

His expression remains serious. "When are you two moving into this apartment?"

"I'm moving in this fall. I can get a roommate until—"

He shakes his head. "No, if she wants to move in with you, she should. I like the idea of her having someone to look after her."

"Oh." I wasn't expecting him to ask me to move in with his twenty-year-old daughter, but I'm not going to complain. "I agree."

"As for the wedding, if you need to elope in order to afford it, I understand. Obviously, I have nothing to contribute financially—"

"Mr. Hayes, please don't think about that. My mom doesn't have a daughter, and I can assure you will be thrilled to pay for a wedding and fight with Dillon over every detail."

"Best of luck to your mom." He smiles and offers his hand again. "Take care of her, okay?"

I'm way too eager when I shake his hand. "Yes, sir. Thank you."

He squeezes my hand tighter when I try to let go. My palm is getting slick again. Now I know where Dillon's commanding personality comes from. "I'm serious, son. She doesn't have a stable thing in her life. You have to be that for her."

"Of course."

"You may never leave her. You may never hurt her. And if I find out you did either—"

"I never will."

He snickers and releases my hand. "I know, Michael. Relax." His arms cross on the table. "Besides, we both know Dillon is the one you should be afraid of." Before I can agree, he says, "Have you ever met someone who crossed her?"

I search my brain for a moment. "No, I don't think I have, actually."

"That's because she ruined them."

TWENTY-THREE

Estlyn

"SORRY. DIDN'T MEAN TO wake you."

What the hell is a cop doing in my room? My eyes immediately dart to his belt. No holster. No gun. His hands are behind his back. He might be holding it there.

"Dillon Collins, right?"

Shit. I don't answer.

"I'm Officer Bennett. I pulled your Uber driver over?"

How could I forget? Now that it's light, I can see he's not much older than I am, maybe thirty. His eyes are a bright blue under his short, dark hair. His shoulders and chest are broad, but his gut isn't as lean as duty probably prefers.

"Your face stuck in my mind tonight, but I couldn't figure out where I recognized you from. Then, after the EMTs took you, I ran you through the system." One hand stays behind his back as he points at me with the other. "You were the eyewitness in the Michael Bishop case."

I don't nod, and I don't move my hands. They're above the blankets. He can see them, right?

"I was there—that night, I mean. Not when it happened, but I was called to the scene after. I, um…" His throat struggles to roll as he swallows. "Look, I'm not going to pretend I know what you went through or anything like that, but do you know the name Luther Bennett? I don't know why you would," Bennett rambles, "he's been out of the headlines for twenty years…"

His eyes light with surprise when I nod. Of course I know the name. I know every case like Michael's in California from the last thirty years.

Bennett's voice is soft when he says, "Okay. Well, Luther was my stepdad. Raised me and my brothers since I was three."

Holy shit.

His eyebrows knit together as he shakes his head. "No one on the force ever apologized or even acknowledged our loss. And then, tonight, I realized you probably never got an apology, either."

Okay, what is happening?

"Dillon, I can't begin to tell you how sorry I am for what happened that night with Michael. This is too little and five years too late, but…" Both his arms swing in front of him, and he looks down at a stuffed animal in his hands. "I was going to bring you flowers because you're sick.

Then I realized flowers die, and you've probably had enough of that shit. So, um—God, this is so weird, but when kids come through the station because they're victims or when they see a parent or someone else killed, we give them one of these to hold and play with while we question them." His hands are uncertain as he presents to me what looks like the softest little lion ever created. "Then they take them home. Or," he shrugs, "wherever they go because most of them don't go home."

He sighs, then continues to talk in an attempt to calm his nerves. He's nervous. *He's* nervous? Because of *me*?

"And I know you're not a kid and you weren't then, but I saw this lion and thought it should be yours." He's growing more uncomfortable as he blathers, rubbing his stubbled chin with three fingers and looking down instead of at me. "I guess I thought of you since lions are fierce and resilient. And, if the police had done something even as simple as this when we lost my dad, it would have meant a lot to me." He sighs with regret and adds, "God, this is so trite, I shouldn't—"

I reach out and take it from his hand. Tears puddle in my lids as I stroke the lion with my thumbs and squish it between my fingers. It's somehow even softer than it looked. My eyes don't venture from it when I whisper, "Thank you."

"May I?" He points to the chair Dean had previously occupied. I nod, though I have no idea why he wants to sit there. "Do the doctors know what happened to you tonight?"

I nod.

"Are you going to be okay?"

I nod once more.

His head bobs forward and back. "I'll let you get some sleep."

As he stands, I blurt out, "Do you like *Fresh Prince*?" I don't know why I want him to stay, but I do. I glimpse the ring on his finger and realize he probably needs to get home to his wife, probably a couple kids, too. They should be his priority, not me.

He relaxes back into the chair. "Everyone likes *Fresh Prince*."

I nod and turn the volume up a notch. My lungs and chest ease as I continue to massage and fidget with the fuzzy little lion in my hands.

Bennett's right. A stuffed animal in exchange for Michael is triter than offering me shit in his hand. But him remembering Michael isn't. Him visiting me in the hospital unarmed isn't. Him apologizing for something no one else did isn't.

I'll take the lion.

I don't know when my eyelids finally give in to my fatigue, but it's light when they recover. Bennett is gone, the little lion he gave me is tucked in my arm, and Linus is asleep on my bed with his hand on my stomach, his face an inch from mine.

TWENTY-FOUR

Cal

A PANICKED WHIR OF alarms wakes me. I jerk upright to check on Estlyn, but she isn't in the hospital bed with me anymore. A nurse bursts through the door, then calms when he sees the EKG is freaking out because no one is hooked up to it.

"Do you know where she is?"

I shake my head.

The nurse pushes some button on the monitor to shut it up, then leaves. I reach for my phone to call Estlyn when I see half a dozen missed calls and a handful of messages from Erin.

Hey, someone called me from UCLA Medical Center trying to get ahold of you. Is everything okay?

Who's in the hospital?

Is it your mom again?

A few hours later, *I'm worried about you.*

Why would Estlyn have Erin's number? Or know who she was or how she was connected to me? Wait, Estlyn was sedated when Dean called me. Maybe Dean knows Erin somehow. But why would Dean know Erin had my number? I text her back, *Hey, sorry. Chaotic night. My mom's fine. My friend had some kind of a heart attack. Who called you?*

She texts back right away. *Oh my God, is he okay? Some nurse called. He wouldn't say who the patient was, just that they needed your number.*

Yeah, she's fine. Thanks for doing that.

Sure.

Yikes. A one-word text ending with a period? Don't think that she liked that my friend is a *she*. *Well, I didn't like that you fucked my dad in our bed because you didn't want to risk the role he offered you. I know, I know. #TimesUp and all. I'm going to hell. But, Erin. Really? You didn't have to choose a part over your self-respect. Or over your boyfriend of five years.*

"Morning." I sit up on the bed to see Estlyn walk in. She's in sweats and a T-shirt tied at her hips. The fabric is loose, but thin enough to see the pads and wires still taped to her chest. Her smooth hair is brushed in front of her left shoulder.

"To hell with the hospital gown?"

She points her toes. "But not the socks. Imma steal some of these. Want any?"

I smirk. "No, I'm okay. Hey, do you know how the hospital got my ex's number?"

An uneasy laugh shakes from her chest. "What?"

"She texted me saying a nurse asked for my number, then Dean called me."

She shrugs. "That's awkward. I'm sorry."

"No, it's okay. Just didn't know you guys knew her."

"I don't. But, Dean's in the industry and knows *everyone*. Maybe he made some calls until he found someone who could get him your number."

Taking her hand, I tug her to sit on the bed next to me. "How are you feeling?"

She rolls her eyes. "I'm fine. Ready to get out of here. I hate hospitals."

"But this one has a wittle wion," I say as I crawl the stuffed animal up her shoulder. She breathes half a laugh, then takes it from me. "You should lie down."

"I'm seriously okay."

Ignoring her protest, I guide her to the pillow, then pick her legs up onto the mattress. I find the EKG cord, then raise her shirt to connect it to the one on her chest. "There." I lie down, facing her. "Now the machine doesn't say you're dead." I twist a lock of her dark hair in my fingers.

"I must like you or something."

She does? Really? "Yeah?"

"I don't let anyone touch my hair."

I pull my hand away to rest it on my thigh. "Est, you should have told me."

149

She finds my hand, pulling it over to cover her breast with it. To clarify, that's where her hair is falling over her chest. "I like it."

"Okay," I whisper.

"Just don't ever get it wet, motherfucker."

A laugh explodes against the roof of my mouth. "Never."

As I play with her hair, I caress her boob through the thin cotton of her shirt. Her eyes close with a contented breath when I trace a circle around her nipple, her fingers moving to my chest to draw gentle squiggles over my torso.

"Can I ask you something?"

"Sure."

"Is this way too fast for you?"

She opens her dark eyes to mine. "What? The fact that you're going to spend a week living in my house as my caregiver after we met only four days ago for what was supposed to be a one-night stand?"

I smile. "That sums it up."

"Is it too fast for you?"

"No. I volunteered, remember?"

"Yeah, but why? You're in that super fun rebound phase I've heard so much about."

"Heard so much about? You've never rebounded?"

"I've never gone through a breakup."

"What?"

"Aren't you supposed to fuck a bunch of girls

to get over your ex?"

"You sound like Elliot."

"He wants you to fuck him?"

I laugh, "I'm hard to resist."

"Linus, I mean, you were with your ex for five years. How many girls have you even been with?"

I wince a little. "Two."

"Including me?"

The embarrassed cringe deepens when I nod.

Her hand pats, then cups, my cheek. "Aw, you're so sweet and innocent."

I push her hand from my face and snicker. "Shut up."

"Should you really spend the week vegging out with me when you could be hooking up with a new girl each night?"

Hold on. "Dean warned me you might do this."

Her eyes narrow. "Do what?"

"Estlyn, you're not getting out of someone taking care of you this week. You're not going back to work."

She grows defensive when she justifies, "I'm just looking out of for you and your evolutionary needs to bang an endless line of hot women."

"That's not an evolutionary need!" I chuckle and add, "Look, I just want to make sure you're okay with me staying with you. I don't want you to think I'm trying to make us more than we are."

"And what are we?"

Good question. "Maybe we could be exclusive this week. Sort of a trial run."

"Like, you'll be my boyfriend?"

"For the week."

"Sure. I can be your girlfriend for the week."

Girlfriend. That word means I'll get to go home with Estlyn and sleep beside her every night and keep my toothbrush in her bathroom and leftovers from our dates in her fridge. I'll get to ask invasive questions about her family and ex-boyfriends and find out her annoying quirks like if she flosses in the living room or bites her nails. I'll get to fight with her about how she works too hard and needs to take it easy and listen to her doctor. I'll see how pretty she is without her makeup every morning and how curly her hair is when it air dries.

What the hell is wrong with me? Let's try this again.

Girlfriend. I'll have regular access to a pussy. That sounds healthier, right?

Estlyn closes her eyes against the pillow. "It'll be like *Pretty Woman*, except you're the cheap hooker."

I stroke her cheek down to her jaw. "Okay, but you owe me three grand and a Rodeo-Drive shopping spree."

"Only three grand? You should adjust for inflation." She yawns and closes her eyes.

I bend to the foot of the bed and pull the sheet

and blanket over us. When I cuddle her against my chest, I ask, "Now that you're my girlfriend and I've told you my number, what's yours?"

"Two," she breathes against my neck.

"Including me?"

She nods.

How is that possible? And how am I one of them?

TWENTY-FIVE

Estlyn

I'M GOING TO KILL Dean. I'm going to strangle his pretty little neck, then bash his thick head of hair in with a brick. Then I'm going to take my key back.

Linus brought me home from the hospital this afternoon. It took less than two minutes for me to discover my tablet and laptop missing and the following note on my counter:

Bitch,

I set up an automated response in your work email explaining that you would respond when you were back in the office at the end of the month. Don't worry, I sent it to every unopened email in your inbox as well. I also reached out to the clients of your three open cases and told them you needed to take a four-week medical leave.

On the counter is your phone for the next four weeks—your ONLY phone.

That phone, by the way, is a pay-as-you-go burner. All it does is text and call. No internet. No data. No email. It's useless.

Enjoy your vacation.

Love,
Dean

Ps. I'm convinced that your condition will vastly improve once you're gettin' it on the regular. Five years of celibacy is plain bad for your health. On that note, enjoy the bag of goodies you paid for with your poker earnings.

Asshole. I pull the tissue paper out of the pink-striped bag. "Oh, God," I whine. It's worse than I thought. There's a slutty, lace bodysuit—which I expected from the pink bag—but there's also a vibrator, massage oil, a copy of the *Kama Sutra*, and two twelve-packs of condoms. Dean thinks I'm going to need twenty-four condoms in seven days? What kind of ho does he think I am?

I have the massage oil in one hand and the *Kama Sutra* in the other when I feel Linus's arms slip around my waist and his face bury in my neck.

"I thought you were supposed to take it easy—do nothing that would get your heartrate up."

Leaning my head back against his shoulder, I feel a shiver each time he kisses my neck. "You

155

think a lot of yourself."

Linus takes my earlobe between his lips, then whispers, "Go sit on the couch and pick out something for us to binge-watch. I'll bring our lunch over."

I curl up in the chaise portion of the couch, settling in to search Netflix. I'm clicking through the "Popular on Netflix" titles when I stumble upon *When We Fall*. I've actually never seen this show despite working so hard to destroy the director and star. Oh, and sleeping with one of the ex-writers.

"Hey, which episodes did you write?"

Linus sets the sandwiches we grabbed on the way home down on the coffee table. "Let's not watch this."

"Why not? Because your ex?"

"No, because—" He covers his face with his hands and groans. "Because I don't like people seeing what I write."

"What? But you're a *writer*. That's your job. That'd be like me saying I don't like people listening to me lie." I wink, and he laughs.

"That's why I'm in screenwriting. Few people go to the movies or watch a show because of the writer. If I wanted to be connected to my work, I'd be a novelist."

"Aww." I puppy-dog my lip. "You're shy."

"Or, I got fired from my job and have a realistic view of my abilities."

"Linus, no offense, but that's bullshit."

"What?"

"I read one of the screenplays you had me forward to my friend."

"Excuse me?"

"Yeah, the biographical sketch of E. E. Cummings that highlighted his inability to sustain a traditional relationship despite writing such whimsically romantic poetry. I loved how you begged the question of whether art is what we experience or what we long for but can never have."

He stares at me a moment, apparently unsure what to do with my analysis of his writing. "Right..." he says, then hesitates. "And if the best art arises from those who feel the vastness of that gap between the perfection they want and the reality of what they can achieve."

"Art inspired by the disappointed idealist."

"Yeah." He nods.

"*When We Fall* it is."

"Estlyn, please," he entreats, his hand on mine. I realize now that he doesn't want me to see the director's name, that he shares the last half of it.

I nod and give him the remote. "You pick." He browses the series and movies until he hovers over a show a beat longer than the others. I know he wants to watch that one, but he's too embarrassed to select it. "I'm a season behind on

Jane the Virgin. Have you ever seen it?"

He chuckles and says, "I'm a season behind, too."

My burner phone buzzes on the coffee table a few minutes into the show. It's a Lancaster area code. I hit talk and listen to the recording, "This is a collect call from," and then my dad's voice says, "Alexander Hayes." The automated voice returns and continues, "an inmate at California State—"

I press *1* to accept. After one ring tone, I'm connected with an unnecessarily worried-sick voice. "Dillon?"

I'm breezy when I answer, "Hey, Dad. How's your weekend shaping up?"

"Dillon. Destiny. Hayes. Don't you *dare* act like you didn't just scare the shit out of your father. What happened?"

"That depends." I nibble on my thumbnail as I ask, "How much do you know?"

"I know that you passed out in the back of a car. I know that you were in the hospital last night and they were monitoring your heart."

"I just had some kind of panic attack. But I'm home now. Back to normal."

"Dean said it was a heart attack. Those are two vastly different things."

"Now, that's not fair. You didn't tell me you knew that."

"Which one was it?"

158

"It was—"

"—And *don't* you lie to me."

I huff. "I had a cardiac event called stress cardiomyopathy. They said my heart sustained no damage and that I'll be fine after I take it easy for a few days."

"That sounds like bullshit. Let me talk to Dean."

"Dean's not here."

"You're alone? You can't be by yourself if—"

"No, no, I'm not alone. I have a friend staying with me this week."

"What friend?"

"Cal."

"Cal? I don't know any Cal."

"I met him Tuesday."

"Dillon," he scolds and lowers his voice, "is he an escort?"

"No, Dad!" He really thinks I have so few friends that I hired an escort to help me as I recover?

"Then what does he do?"

"He's a writer."

"What does he write?"

"Television and movies."

"I almost prefer the escort story."

Literature snob. "He's also a part-time bartender."

"Is he any good?"

"At bartending or writing?"

"How hard is bartending?"

"Well, he makes a mean Old Fashioned and has mastered period-specific dialogue. Does that answer your question?"

"Is he straight?"

"Jesus, Dad. That's neither relevant nor your business."

"He is, isn't he?"

"Why does his sexual orientation matter?" Linus glances at me with a confused smirk. I shake my head and roll my eyes to dismiss him from our conversation.

"He's not a friend! He's a straight boy!"

"I can have male friends who aren't gay."

"Let me talk to him."

"Dad—"

"*Now*, Dillon."

TWENTY-SIX

Cal

ESTLYN GROANS AND HANDS the burner to me. "My dad wants to talk to you."

"Okay…" I put the phone to my ear, expecting a voice just as intimidating as Estlyn's, but, of course, lower and more intense because he's her dad, and girlfriends'—even temporary ones'—dads are frightening. "Hello?"

"Hi Cal, it's Mr. Hayes." Oh. He sounds less terrifying than Estlyn's dad should. Also, by his last name, he must be her biological dad. So, he's not dead. Why did she say he was in hell?

"Hi, Mr. Hayes, how are you?"

"I'm worried about my baby girl. She's a compulsive liar."

Good to know.

"Can you tell me how she's actually doing?"

"Hang on." I stand up and head for the balcony, so I can rat out Estlyn without her knowing. When I close the sliding door behind me, I answer, "She told you the truth except she needs four weeks to

161

rest, not a few days."

"Okay, anything else?"

"Yeah, the doctor said it was induced by some sort of emotional stress. I guess it's called 'broken heart syndrome.' They want her to see a psychologist, but she refused."

"That sounds about right. Listen, Cal, seeing a psychologist is going to be a lost cause, so don't even bother. But, are you able to stay with her for the next four weeks? I know that's a lot to ask, but—"

"No, of course, I can."

"Okay. Don't let her answer the door or drive herself."

"I won't, but is she in danger or something?"

There's a beep on the line, and then her dad says, "Hey, Cal, I gotta go. Thanks."

Before I can reply, the line goes dead. When I close the sliding door behind me, Estlyn says, "Shoulda said you were gay."

I flop on the couch beside her. "Why?"

"He wants you to stay longer, doesn't he?"

"Four weeks. How'd you—"

"God, I'm sorry. He thinks I'm a spinster."

"You're twenty-five."

"I turn twenty-six in the fall."

"Oh," I tease, "well, twenty-six and no ring would make you an old maid."

"You really don't have to stay."

"No, it's fine." I wrap my arm around her.

"We can stretch this trial run out to a month. But you'll have to pay me more."

She laughs against my neck, then presses her lips there. Her fingers find the button on my jeans. "Then you'll have to put out more."

Her hand is already making me hard when I whisper, "Tomorrow. You're taking it easy today."

"Fine," she sighs and pulls her hand from my boxers.

I reach for the remote and notice something from the hospital on the coffee table. "What's that doing here?" I ask as I point to the stuffed lion positioned to face the television.

She shrugs. "I wanted someone to hang out with while you were on the phone."

TWENTY-SEVEN

Cal

I'D FORGOTTEN HOW INCREDIBLE it is to live with a woman. There's always shampoo, body wash, and conditioner in the shower, which, by the way, is not outlined with black mold. The toilet doesn't look like a jellyfish died upside down in it. Her refrigerator has produce and dairy—some of it is even *organic*. The kitchen sink and garbage never overflow. And I've slept between a top *and* a fitted sheet for three nights in a row now. Yes, one of those nights was in the hospital, but it still counts.

Lately, I've been living with a guy who owns only four real dishes and one bottle of some kind of soap in his shower that I assume he uses for everything. And he doesn't care about having a real career or the fact that he's never had more than nine-hundred dollars in the bank or that he sleeps on a mattress with just a blanket and no sheets.

I actually have to applaud him. I've never

gotten the hang of bachelor life, but Elliot's great at it, especially the casual sex part. Apparently, I'm incapable of casual sex. But, that's okay. Estlyn seems to be, too.

I've learned more about her in three days than I did about Erin in our first three months of dating. Besides the fact that she's a restless, Type-A workaholic who acts like sick leave is torture, I've noticed Estlyn has some behaviors that can only be described as... hella weird. Not the kind of weird where I'm scared for my well-being. Not even the kind of weird that makes me want to stop seeing her. Just an inexplicable kind of weird.

I've turned it into a game: Condoms Used vs. New Strange-Ass Behavior. The current score is four to three, Team Condom in the lead. If I were to record and study Estlyn's actions scientist-style—which I don't because I'm not a creep—the journal entries would go something like this.

4:40 AM, Saturday: Estlyn talks in her sleep at the hospital. When she does, her EKG reports such elevated levels of stress that alarms start blaring, causing a nurse to rush in to check on her. Subject does not wake; instead continues to mumble or loudly contest that her case should be thrown out because Monroe obtained his evidence illegally.

1:51 AM, Sunday: Subject is no longer asleep in her bed, but is instead attempting to pick the lock of her file cabinet with a bobby pin. After eleven minutes of unsuccessful locksmithing, she pours a glass of white wine and retires to the couch, where she cries for six minutes before I join her with the excuse that the living room light woke me. When I ask her what is wrong, the subject replies, "Why would you think anything is wrong?" She then turns on the television and climbs on top of me. Subject kisses me and tries to pull my underwear off. I tell her I do not want to have sex, I want to make sure she is okay. She tells me she is always okay and that I should go back to bed. I do not go back to bed. After three glasses of wine, she bawls again for ten minutes until she falls asleep slouched against my chest. I cover her with a blanket, and we sleep the rest of the night on the couch.

2:27 AM, Monday: Subject has built some kind of sheet structure between the coffee table and couch with a dining chair bracing the middle. I peek under said fort to find her lying down, surrounded by couch pillows and reading one of the books we bought yesterday by flashlight. Upon closer inspection, subject is sharing pillow with a stuffed lion propped up to give the illusion that it is reading over her shoulder.

I knock on the seat of the chair.

"Come in," she answers, then turns the page.

After I crawl under the sheet, I lie on my back beside her. I glance at her face, but her eyes don't leave the book. Since I interrupted her weird ritual last night, I figure I should respect this one.

So instead of interacting with her, I watch the breeze coming through the sliding door ripple the sheet above us like water.

I'm dozing off when she finally says, "My dad taught me to do this."

"To read?"

"In a tent." She drops the open book to her chest. "I had some focus issues as a kid. And poor reading comprehension." Her face turns my way and breathes a soft laugh. "Books were so fucking boring. So, my dad started reading to me in a tent to kind of tune out the distractions. He told me that when I went into the tent, the rest of the world didn't exist, that I was walking into the world of that book. Those characters were the only people who were real. What they said and felt and did were the only things that mattered." She picks up the book again.

"What world are you in right now?"

"Rural town in the Midwest where a teenage boy slaughtered his family in the eighties."

"Yikes."

Her eyes cut to mine. "Or did he?"

I burst out laughing. "Is this some kind of normal thing I missed as I kid?"

"I have no idea. Rory didn't know about it, so maybe it's not normal. But he didn't really have a parent to build a reading tent for him."

"That's sad."

She shrugs.

"What happened to them?"

"His mom abandoned him. Cops found her a couple years later after she OD'd. Heroin."

"God."

She nods, still apparently reading.

I turn onto my side and prop my head up in my hand. "When was the last time you slept? I mean, really slept? A whole night?"

She scrunches her forehead to think, then turns the page. "Five years, probably."

God. "Estlyn…" I say as I take the book from her.

"Linus, the tent has rules." She reaches for the book, but I pull it back. "I'm sure you're familiar with suspension of disbelief. Reality doesn't enter the tent."

"Why has it been five years?"

"This is a perfect example of an outside-of-tent topic."

"Say no more." I hand her the book and crawl out from under the sheet. She's reading again when I grab both of her ankles and drag her out.

"What the fuck, Linus?"

She struggles, but she's so light and slender and sucks at defending herself that I slide her out of the tent with ease. For how tough she is, she's delicate enough to throw over my shoulder.

She hits my back and kicks the air. "This is also against tent rules!"

"We aren't in the tent anymore." I drop her

onto the bed and flip her over to her stomach. I straddle her ass and start kneading her shoulders and upper back. "You're not going to get better if you stay up every night drinking and reading about kids murdering their families."

"*One* kid," she murmurs as my hands move beneath the fabric of her tank top to better knead the muscles between her shoulder blades. I catch her glossy eyes glaring at me before she closes them. Good. Maybe this will get her to sleep. My fingers stop massaging her long enough to pull the hem of her shirt up, getting it out of the way, and she stretches her arms over her head to let me take it off her. I warm the body oil I find on her nightstand between my hands before pressing them into her back again. That's when I notice a tear trickle over the bridge of her nose.

I stroke her hair away from her face and whisper, "What's wrong?"

She replies with calculated breaths, the kind someone uses to keep a quiet tear from turning into untamable crying. She never answers my question, so I continue massaging her back.

I don't know exactly how long it takes her to fall asleep, but after half an hour of this, she's definitely out. I shut off the flashlight in the living room, then crawl under the covers to fall asleep with her. It's not yet dawn when her voice awakens me.

"You shouldn't have told him. You didn't have to tell him," she mumbles over and over.

TWENTY-EIGHT

Michael

FIVE YEARS AGO

THE MATTRESS DIPS AND rises for the fourth time tonight. I'm not even counting the times Dillon has simply tossed around, these are just the times she's gotten out of our bed.

Our bed.

We moved into our overpriced one-bedroom apartment two weeks ago, the day after her last final. I haven't proposed yet, but there's plenty of time after the trial ends to do that. She has enough going on right now.

My eyes open to the sight of Dillon sitting on the edge of the mattress in my Clippers T-shirt, her legs dangling over the side. "Baby," I murmur, "you can't sway the jury telepathically."

She rubs the back of her neck, then rolls it around. "Three days means they're leaning toward acquittal, right?"

I've stopped answering this question. There's no good way to. I could try to give her hope, but she won't grasp it. This is the second time she's

170

waited for a jury to condemn or release her father, and it didn't end well last time.

Once I sit up, I scoot behind her to surround her legs with mine. "Here." I replace the hand on her neck with my own, massaging the muscles strung tight between her shoulders and head. "Can we try to have some fun tomorrow? Take your mind off things?"

She grumbles, "Fun? Do we have to?"

"Yes. It's the weekend. They won't be deliberating, so there's nothing even to think about." My lips meet the curve of her neck. "And Grandma's having a barbecue. Everyone's going to be there." I hug her, rocking us side to side with each idea I add—to the right, "You can win all of my cousins' money in poker," to the left, "then we'll eat too much and get trashed," to the right again, "and lose everything we won back to my cousins on the Lakers' game. What do you say?"

"Your grandma hates me."

"She doesn't hate you, she just…"

"Doesn't like that I'm a different color than you."

I sigh. "That doesn't mean she doesn't like you. Just doesn't like you for me."

"That's the same thing."

"She'll come around. We'll make her a pie and say it was your idea. That'll win her over."

"Oh yeah. From what I remember, pie ended

apartheid." With a sigh, she leans into my chest and mutters, "Fine. I'll start slicing apples."

"It's four in the morning."

She pushes off my thighs to stand, then turns with her hands on her hips. "Do you have something else in mind that I should do?"

I snatch her hand and pull her down to the bed with me. She giggles and shoves against me as I cover her face and neck with kisses. I stick my tongue out and clutch her against me. She flinches away.

"Don't you *dare* lick me!"

"You like when I lick you some places."

"Ew!"

"What? Should I not do that anymore?" She slaps my arms before I slobber all over her cheek.

"Is annoyingness attached to the Y chromosome or something?"

"If I lick you in a place you like, will it help you be able to sleep after?"

"It doesn't matter if it does. You owe me now."

I roll her on her back and kiss her as my hand slides between her thighs. I press her leg to the mattress, then whisper, "Okay. Try to sleep."

TWENTY-NINE

Cal

"GOD, SHE'S DRIVING ME batshit crazy."

I laugh and pour Dean another whiskey as he complains. He spent the day with Estlyn yesterday, and Rory is with her today.

"She's burning through a lot of tactics to get me to cave." Dean's finger and eyebrow raise, resolute. "But I won't, Cal. She tried calling me every minute of every day, so I put her on my 'Do Not Disturb' list. Then she called my work phone, but joke's on her because I just ignore it until my office mate gets so annoyed with the ringing that she picks it up. Estlyn can listen to Tonya bitch about her maybe-cheating husband all day. Gives me a break." His eyes widen, and both hands fly to his mouth. "Oh, shit. She's not trying to get me to cave. She's drumming up business!"

"Is she a divorce lawyer?"

He throws back his whiskey with a grimace and shakes his head. How do I still not know what she does?

I glance past Dean's shoulder as a man close to my dad's age takes nervous steps closer and closer to Dean. Once he's in his space, he taps his back. Dean whips around to face him.

"Excuse me, are you Dean Martinez?"

His eyes are full of suspicion as he studies the stranger. "Um, why?"

"It's Dwayne. We've been chatting on Match. com and are supposed to meet up here at seven."

Dean's shoulders slouch and his expression turns sympathetic. "Sweetie, you've been catfished."

"Been what?"

"I'm Dean, but I'm not on any dating site."

"Really? Because"—the older gentleman displays Dean's dating profile on his phone for him—"you're right here."

Dean grabs the phone and starts scrolling through the profile. "'Male seeking male, any race or religion, age fifty-five and older.' Seriously? 'I love me a sweaty old gay with that curly, salt-and-pepper chest hair. The longer and curlier the better. I want it poking above those top shirt buttons. Oh, yeah, let it blow in the wind while we drive down PCH in your Lincoln sedan with the windows cracked. In search of someone I can raise a family of hypoallergenic, small-breed dogs with; someone who doesn't have all their original joints. I'm so over all these sexy twinks who just want me for my hot bod. Looking for a real man to settle down with, preferably in a gay-friendly, fifty-five-and-older community."'

I can't help but give Dean's blind date a once-over. The poor guy is buttoning the second-to-top button over his ungroomed, grey chest hair as Dean reads. His upper lip looks like the outside of a cold drink on a hot day.

Dean gives the man back his phone, then drops his forehead into his hand. "Cal, did you let Estlyn go to the library?"

"Um…"

He glares at me. "Cal?"

"Yes?" How was I supposed to know she'd use a computer to catfish unsuspecting old gays?

He turns to the humiliated older gentleman with confident compassion. "Sorry, hon. My friend set you up. Best of luck to finding a man half your age to raise that family of dogs with." Dean sends him off with a pat on the shoulder.

I pour him another whiskey before he can even ask for it. Dean points at me while holding his glass. "The secret, Cal, is not to engage. She's like a toddler. When she throws a tantrum, you just have to calmly put her in timeout, drink hard liquor, and plot your revenge for when she least expects it." He swallows his drink whole, then says, "I'm off to the loo. More wisdom when I come back."

Chuckling, I drop the glasses in the nearly full bus bin. I'm not sure if I haven't known

175

Estlyn long enough to be that annoyed with her, or if she's taking it easy on me. Or maybe it's because she's so fucking hot and all her quirks intrigue me more than frustrate me. Or maybe I should be on high alert for an elderly widow with a recent hip replacement to invite me to an early bird dinner.

When I return from the back with the empty bin, I freeze halfway to the bar at the sight of Erin. The two trains I'm usually hit with when I see her don't flatten me the way they usually do. Not that getting hit by a train is ever pleasant, but it might not be fatal this time.

"Hey." Erin smiles, rubbing her arms like she's trying to warm the nervousness out of herself.

"Hey. Do you want a drink?"

She shakes her head. "No, I just wanted to, uh…" She looks down at the counter. "Actually, a glass of chardonnay, please."

"Sure." I reach into the wine fridge for the bottle, then set a glass in front of her. "Have you heard about your job?"

"Yeah, that's what I stopped by to tell you, actually. The producers fired your dad."

That fills me with a joy so pure, I don't even care that I'm going to hell because of it. I focus on the wine pouring into the glass to conceal my satisfied smirk. "So, does that mean you have a job still?"

She takes the glass from my hand and sighs.

"I don't know. Netflix might be dropping the show."

"Shit. Why?"

"Taylor got arrested, so..."

"Again?"

She laughs. "He's out on bail, but apparently the police got ahold of a video of him screwing some teenage girl. *Again.*"

I roll my eyes. "How narcissistic do you have to be to film yourself having sex that many times?"

"Pretty damn narcissistic." She grins and adds, "Anyway, my agent's booking me some auditions." She twists the stem of her wine glass between her fingers. "What about you?"

"Oh..." I condense the *I'm staying with a terrifying, hot-as-fuck lawyer whose brain might be slightly broken. She set me up with an agent* update to: "I got an agent. She loves my screenplay, and has a couple producers she thinks will be interested in it."

Her eyes brighten. "Damn, Cal, you land on your feet."

"Erin, I'm homeless and working twenty hours a week at a bar."

"Yeah, about that..." She sighs, then shuts her eyes. "Cal, the lease on our apartment is up next month, and"—she winces—"I want to renew it."

"Okay?"

"With you."

"Oh."

Dean slides back onto his stool. "Estlyn claims no involvement in the old-gay scheme." Then he points at me and adds, "You should know that she's a pathological liar. Luckily, she has a tell." It's only then he notices that I'm in the middle of a conversation with Erin. "Oh, God, I'm so rude."

He taps the bar twice and stands to leave, but Erin puts her hand on his arm. "Wait. Dean, right?"

This is the first time I've ever seen Dean ruffled. He's acting more on-edge because Erin recognizes him than when that poor catfished man did. "Yeah," he affirms through a shaky grin, "and you're Erin, the rising star that took down Ron Calloway."

Erin takes a miniature bow at his praise. "Thanks again for writing that article."

"Yeah, girl, no problem. Now, if you'll excuse me, I have a bitchy friend whose dating life awaits to be sabotaged." Dean winks at me, then makes his way to the door.

Erin spins to me. "How do you two know each other?"

Oh... *fuck.* Lying never works with her, but telling a half-truth works half the time. I'll take those odds. "We have a mutual friend," I say with a shrug. "LA's a small town, you know that." I wipe down the bar. "So, you told Dean the story about my dad? How'd you find him?"

"Oh, he found me, actually."

178

"What?"

"Yeah, it was kind of weird. He called me, told me he worked for TMZ, and said he had heard some rumors about Ron abusing his relationships with actresses and asked for comment."

"He called you? How'd he get your number?"

"God…" Leaning back, she sighs. "I don't know. He works at TMZ. They do whatever they need to for a story, right?"

"Yeah, I guess. Estlyn said he was well-connected."

"Estlyn?"

Shit. See, this is why any girl I date has my guaranteed fidelity. I'm too damn stupid to get away with cheating. Or careless. Two sides to the same coin. "Yeah, she's our mutual friend."

She nods. "How long have you been sleeping with her?"

I would say, *Excuse me? Who are you to accuse me of screwing someone else? How is that any of your business, fatherfucker?* But she's not accusing me. There's jealousy in her tone, but no indigence. Her eyebrows cinch together as she looks up at me with that anxious sense of loss, that realization that she got here too late. And she just asked me to move back in with her. She should know my answer.

"Erin, I'm not ready to commit to moving back in with you."

"Has it been longer than a month, Cal?"

Okay, now she's being a bitch. I scoff and grip the edge of the bar. My head dips between my locked arms and shakes in disbelief at her accusation. Although, I'm actually thrilled she just said that. Because Estlyn might talk in her sleep and build tent forts—which, by the way, I'm starting to find endearing—but she doesn't see the worst in me. The opposite, in fact. She assumed I was a talented writer before she even offered me a connection to her friend at WME. She assumed I was good in bed when she first saw me. She assumed I would fit in with her friends when she brought Rory and Dean to the Dive. Besides my crippling post-breakup fear that I'm going to lose any girl who gets near me, Estlyn gives me confidence.

I lift my head and smile at her—a genuine smile. "Thank you, Erin, for asking. Because now I remember I didn't leave you because you fucked my dad. I left you because you treated me like shit."

"Cal, come on. It's a legitimate question."

"No, it's not, because I'm not you. I don't cheat. If you want to resign the lease, be my guest. Just take my name off it."

Erin chugs the rest of the wine, then drops a few bills on the counter before storming out.

I pull my phone out of my pocket, go to messages, and type a text to Estlyn.

Can't wait to see you!

I erase it and try again.

Hope you're feeling well. Need me to bring home anything after my shift?

THIRTY

Estlyn

"**YOU'RE SURE IT'S UNTRACEABLE,** right?"

Rory pops the cap off his second bottle of Corona, which I bought specifically because I knew he was coming over. "Est, as far as seventeen-year-old me knew, yes." He takes a swig of his beer. "I thought we went over this last week. Did he reach out again?"

"I wouldn't know because Dean changed the password on my email account."

"Damn, he is thorough."

"No shit. Can you hack into it?"

He nods. "But I won't."

"Fuck you. I hope the beer makes you too bloated to get laid tonight."

He almost spits it out when he laughs. "Look, Est, no one is going to investigate a five-year-old crime, especially after his appeals were rejected, right? And shouldn't the statute of limitations be up for everything we did, anyway?"

"Not embezzlement."

He shrugs. "I doubt they'll charge us."

"The cops are the least of our worries. Monroe could come after us directly."

"You're being paranoid. Didn't they give you Xanax or something. Can you take one?"

Dean interrupts us by knocking his signature beat. He must have forgot his key. He usually just barges in. I check through the peephole before answering—can't be too careful. I swing it open to find Dean leaning one hand against the frame, glowering. More like smoldering because, let's face it, he's fucking hot. "So, should I be expecting any other old men to proposition me? Perhaps at my home or maybe my place of work?" He primps the collar of his jacket, *Grease*-style, as he walks in.

"Dean, you can love whoever you want to love. You know I've never judged."

"Cal will be revoking your library privileges."

I shut the door and lean my back against it. "I don't like your little friendship."

He flops onto the couch and nods at Rory because apparently that's all men need to do to properly greet each other. "Don't worry. I'm not going to the Dive anymore."

"Oh really?"

"His ex showed up."

My stomach sinks. It actually feels heavy. Not because I'm jealous, but because Erin knows Dean, and Dean knows me, and me knows Linus, who was the person Erin showed up at the Dive to see.

"Did you get out of there before she saw you?"

He shakes his head. "I handled it, though. And I don't think Cal suspects you took his emergency contacts."

Yet.

"Oh," Dean continues, "Calloway got fired, Taylor got arrested, and Net—" He stops to glare at me when he realizes I already know everything he's telling me.

"Library," I explain.

"No more. Cal promised to keep you away from computers."

"Oh, please. He's not coming back." I twist off the lid of my beer and kick my feet up on the coffee table.

Rory swipes it from my hand. "You're not supposed to be drinking."

I snatch it back. "Neither are you!"

"What do you mean he's not coming back?" Dean exclaims. "He *has* to. You will die here alone before I have to stay three weeks with you."

Ah, a true friend. "You said his ex-girlfriend was at the bar."

"So?"

"So, were they fighting?"

Dean studies the ceiling before saying, "No."

"Then he probably wants to be with her."

Dean's eyes widen as he turns to Rory. "You

hear this, right?"

Rory rolls his eyes as he tips his beer to his lips.

"Your sister *likes* the boy."

"Don't push it," Rory says, then turns up the volume on the baseball game.

Dean takes my hand. "Honey, I mean this from the bottom of my heart. Are you listening?"

I nod.

"You are, honest to God, the most intolerable person to live with when you aren't working."

"*Please*, don't spare my feelings."

"And this guy volunteered to do that for four weeks. So, either the sex is mind-blowing—"

"It is."

"Nope." Rory shakes his head, his eyes attached to the baseball game. "Just... no."

"Or," Dean continues, "he likes you. Either way," he says, gritting his teeth and pounding his fist against his other palm, "he is *not* abandoning us in our time of need."

"I thought you weren't supposed to have sex right now."

I turn to Rory and shrug. "It's a grey area—medically."

"And it's been too long," Dean adds.

I pull my knees up to my chest and sip my beer, grateful for the distraction of the television, even if it is baseball. But Dean's watching me. I can see him in my periphery.

"Estlyn, there's nothing to feel guilty about. Michael would want you to be happy."

I clear my throat to trick the tears out of falling. "No Michael-talk."

"Why not? You really should after—"

"Dean, I said no."

Rory turns the volume up on the television even more.

THIRTY-ONE

Michael

FIVE YEARS AGO

I SCOOP DILLON UP in my arms to carry her down my grandparents' driveway. She doesn't drink often, and I'm not sure she's ever been drunk before. Tonight, though, she went at it hard. But, hey, she unwound like she needed to, even if she did cross the line from tipsy to sloppy a couple of hours ago. Her arms wrapped around my neck, I can smell the beer on her breath as she sucks my earlobe.

"God, I want to fuck you so bad," she slurs.

"Yeah, you took that getting-trashed idea to a whole 'nother level."

"I can't wait till we get home. Let's get in the back seat."

"Hell, no. We're not having sex in the car in front of my *grandma's* house."

"Then park somewhere else."

I set her feet on the sidewalk by the passenger door. She drops limp from my arms and folds forward when she lands, decorating the cement

187

with puke. *Reason B we're not having sex right now.*

"Ugh…" she moans, leaning her back against the car. "I feel like shit."

"I know, baby." I wipe the vomit from her lip with my sleeve. "Let's get you home."

She gulps a gallon of air, then sobs, "My dad's going to die in a cell."

Oh, boy.

"I should have told the police that day that she fell. Or slipped. Michael, it's all my fault…"

I hold her close and steady her just enough to get her into the passenger seat, then crouch down so I can cup her face in my hands. "Dillon, none of this is your fault. No matter what happens, you are guilty of none of it. Do you understand? Dillon?" Her eyelids droop, and the hand that was holding my wrist drops to her lap. I smile and kiss her forehead before I jog around the front of the car.

We're two blocks from home when red-and-blue lights flash in my rearview mirror. There's that sharp pain through my chest, that anxiety-like a vice around my lungs, as I pull to the curb. I know to watch my speed here. There's an officer with a radar gun here every other day lately. I couldn't have been going more than forty-five in the forty.

The cop climbs off his bulky motorcycle behind me toward my door. Dillon stirs, and her eyelids flutter open when she sees the uniform. She scoots upright at the sight. The officer stoops to see us through the window. "License and registration."

I rest both hands on the steering wheel but don't reach for my glove box or my wallet. I should have had those out already, but we would've had this conversation anyway. "Sir," I look him in the eyes as I say, "I have a license to carry a firearm, and that firearm is in the car."

My pulse skips when his hand moves to his gun and grips his holster. "Where is it?"

"In the center console."

"Okay, don't reach for it."

"Yes, sir." I grip the steering wheel in compliance.

"Get out of the car." When I start to move he adds, "Slowly."

"Yes, sir." My hands tremble as I pivot toward my seat-belt buckle.

Out of the corner of my eye, I see his gun rip from his holster as he shouts, "Don't reach for it! I said don't do it!"

I try to put my hands back in the air, but they don't make it there.

My back slams against my seat like I've been hit across the chest with a bat. It's when I register the pop of the gun and feel the sting of the bullet that I know what happened.

All I can think of is Dillon.

My fingers release my seatbelt as I'm smacked again, this time in the back, when I turn to cover Dillon. There's another crack and burn in my neck as I slump sideways onto her lap. I'm scared as shit that she's going to die because I chose to have a gun, because I thought we'd be safer with it.

I'm a fucking moron.

I'm facing her when I roll to protect her, but my body doesn't cooperate. I just need to know if she's hit. If she's going to be safe. My eyes make the journey to her face.

She's scared sober.

She's screaming.

She's soaked in blood.

And I can't tell if it's mine or hers. *God, don't let it be hers.*

The officer shouts behind me, "Put your hands up!" but his voice is drowning under the blurry sea of red I'm sinking into.

Another crack.

Another sting in my shoulder.

Another scream from the chest in front of mine.

Choking on the hot sludge in my throat, I gasp, "You hit?"

Her eyes don't meet mine. They're darting over my back and chest, then out the driver's window. I'm dizzy as she screams, "He's not going to shoot you, motherfucker! Help!"

I hear some mumbling about a bus behind me, then Dillon repeating, "Baby, you're okay. You're okay. Baby, you're okay."

I feel her hands on my neck, but I can't tell if I can't breathe because I'm choking on blood or because she's putting pressure on the wound. When one of her hands presses into the burning spot on my chest and the other into the one on my back, I realize I'm drowning from within.

Hers is the last voice I hear as my static view fades to black.

"Michael, I love you! Don't you dare close your eyes! Baby, you're okay. You're okay. You will not leave me..."

THIRTY-TWO

Cal

RORY OPENS ESTLYN'S DOOR with one finger over his pursed lips. The TV is on, so I'm not sure why I have to be quiet until he points to Estlyn curled up on the chaise. Asleep. With the lion under her arm.

"How the hell did you do that?" I whisper as I hand him a plastic bag full of Chinese takeout.

Dean turns his head over his arm stretched over the back of the couch. "Like a toddler," he whispers. "Let her wear herself out, confine her to a designated sleeping space, and—again—liquor. Did you get a dozen vegetarian spring rolls?"

Nodding, I hand him the other bag.

As soon as I ease quietly into the seat between him and Estlyn, Dean leans to my ear and asks, "What happened with your ex?"

I shake my head. "She asked if I wanted to move back in," I say, rolling my eyes.

His eyebrows wrinkle, his mouth widening to an *O*. "Shit. Are you?"

Is he joking? "Hell no. Would I be here if I were moving back in with her?"

He softly singsongs, "I told Est you like her."

Estlyn stretches beside me. "Why didn't you wake me up for Chinese?" she asks while trying to tame her smashed-down curls. I love her big curls, the way she throws her hair over one side of her head because she has too much to tuck it behind her ear.

"Hey," I breathe and lean to meet her lips.

She kisses me hard, twisting her fist in the chest of my shirt. Her deep, espresso eyes soften when she pulls away.

"What'd you name him?"

"Who?"

I pick up the little lion and shake it in front of her.

"Oh, *she* is Lioness. Get it?"

"But female lions don't have manes."

"What are you, a zoologist?" Estlyn shoves my chest and reaches for a white paper box. "Thanks for buying dinner."

"Oh, I didn't. I'm keeping receipts of all my expenses to turn into you for reimbursement."

She snickers and cuddles against me before digging into her orange chicken with chopsticks. For a moment, I feel her muscles relax when I drape my arm around her.

The moment is all too brief, interrupted by pounding on the door.

THIRTY-THREE

Estlyn

Five Years Ago

Death is emptiness.

It's an empty apartment with his furniture, with his books and clothes.

It's an empty kitchen that holds his favorite foods.

It's an empty shower with soap I'll never breathe from his skin again.

It's an empty bed with the covers thrown back, the way he left them.

It's an empty embrace, cold where his arms used to surround me.

It's an empty scream that cries to walls that echo but can't hear.

It's an empty ache in my chest, hollow and raging to be filled.

And I swear to God I will fill it.

There was no saving Michael. I knew it when I felt the gushing wound in his neck. No matter how hard I tried, I couldn't stop the bleeding. All I could do was lie to him about it. The ambulance arrived a minute after his heart beat its last. And what a vain beat it was, the blood spilling out of his vessels into my hands and lap and seat.

Michael and I were the eye in the storm of flashing lights and shrieking sirens. EMTs and police surrounded the car. One of them opened the passenger door to the *alleged* crime scene. I didn't snap or shout when I told them all to fuck off, that he was gone, that they couldn't take what was left of him from me. I was no threat to anyone. The officer had already confiscated Michael's gun from the console, not that Michael or I had ever intended to use it.

My fingertips grazed his smooth cheek while it was still warm. As the heat retreated from his skin, I fingered his fade, then twisted the short curls he promised Uncle Will he'd buzz before law school. I never wanted him to buzz them.

I kissed his forehead and his lips. I told him I loved him, that everything would be okay. I told him how full of butterflies I was when he sought me out after debate class to accuse me of cheating. I told him I'd had a crush on him for a couple of weeks by then and was thrilled I'd finally gotten his attention. I told him I was so glad he'd brought an ice cream sandwich to my dorm last May. I asked him what happened to it between the time I fell asleep and woke up. I accused him of eating it, of liking peanut butter cookie and strawberry ice cream but being too much of a stubborn ass to admit it. And every so often, I'd repeat, "It's all going to be okay, baby. I love you, so it's all going to be okay."

His parents arrived at the scene, calm and sober-hearted, shock keeping them from collapsing under the weight of their loss. His mama stooped to the window to leave a kiss on his cool forehead. She took my cheek in her hand—her skin a stark warm compared to Michael's. "It's time to let him go, baby girl."

I shook my head as the tears and snot cascaded down my face. My arms cradled him to my chest as if my warmth could heat his body to life. They couldn't take him away yet. I hadn't told him everything. What if he didn't know how much I loved him? What if he didn't know the magnitude of his strength, of his patience and gentleness and understanding? What if he didn't know that I couldn't breathe in a world where he didn't, in a world where he wasn't allowed to?

If this world has no air for him, it has none I can breathe either.

Dean, one of the few friends I've made during the chaos of the last couple years, met me at the police station with an extra T-shirt of his own for me to change into. Michael's blood had saturated my clothes and caked and cracked on my skin beneath them. Dean lifted my shirt, heavy as chainmail, over my ashen face. Numb, I glanced down at the only remnants of Michael I had—

maroon blood dried on my chest and abdomen. My navel appeared scabbed where it had pooled and crusted as I held him. My body woke from its stunned paralysis when Dean came at me with a wet paper towel.

I batted at him, wailing, "Don't wash him away!"

Dean tossed the paper towel in the trash can and helped me into his clean shirt. He pulled me to him as I wept. The thought that plagued me, that I couldn't push out, was how warm he felt.

Michael would never feel warm again.

Dean held me the same way in his bed that night, knowing I couldn't go home to that apartment without Michael. The next morning, I woke up nauseated and starving and parched from the alcohol still in my body. For sure, I thought, the night before had to have been a terrible dream. The lights and gunshots and screams couldn't have happened. Then I ran my hand over my stomach and felt Michael's blood clotted there. It wouldn't matter if I stayed in bed or got up. Every day would be this nightmare.

I'm back in our apartment now. For the last six weeks, I've been lying on the couch at night instead of in bed. The covers are collecting dust the way Michael left them strewn after he got up on his last morning. I'm careful to leave all of his things the way he did. I've only moved his clothes because I have to wear them; I have to smell what's left of him in them.

Today I have to dress in my own clothes. I have to shower and shave and at least apply mascara. But I refuse to tame my curls. Some are loose, others coiled tight, all of them voluminous and pointing whatever direction they want to. They're not smoothed down my back or contained in an updo like usual. They're big all over my head, defying gravity the way only my natural hair can. I will let them defy.

I will defy.

I push through the doors of the courtroom that has become my father's battlefield the last year. My chin is held high as I face our defeat because, after all this, my dad and I still lost.

Hell, Michael and I lost, too.

Officer Monroe, who shot Michael four times in six seconds, faced a prosecutor, a grand jury, and me just a week after he killed him. I testified to what I saw, heard, and experienced in those six seconds, but I couldn't say what had made Monroe fire his weapon. I'd been too intoxicated.

Officer Monroe was not indicted for homicide. He went home to his family. After six weeks of desk duty, he was put back out into Los Angeles with his gun and badge that gave him permission to pull over and detain and kill whomever he wanted. As long, of course, as those facing the barrel of his gun looked like Michael.

My dad, on the other hand, was convicted

of murder in the second degree, a felony with a minimum sentence of twenty-five years and a maximum of life. Last time, he got life. This time, he won't.

I stand to face the judge when Uncle Will gives me the okay. My hands don't tremble. They hold no paper with an unmemorized speech. I know what I have to say, and I'm confident I won't forget a single piece. Because that's what happens when you lose everything—you lose your fear, too.

"Your Honor, thank you for giving me yet another chance to speak before you today. The last few weeks have been the worst of my life, not just because I lost my father again or because my boyfriend was shot dead in my arms, but because I've learned the truth about what it means to be human.

"I have never been naive. I have known that humanity varied in power, in wealth, and in opportunity. But now I know that we also vary in worth. The sincerity of our words, the morality of our actions, the rightness of our intentions are not measured by our character. No..." I shake my head. "They are measured by the worth our fellow man assigns to us.

"Your Honor, in the past six weeks I have learned my worth and the worth of those I love. My father will return to jail because twenty-four people have now assigned a higher worth to the woman who tormented me than to the man who defended me. My boyfriend died of four bullets to the chest and neck, but no one will face charges because a grand jury decided the one who killed him is worth more than he was."

I pull in my breath to steady myself at the word *was* before I can start again. "Both their lives hold my voice in common. I testified to the death of my mom, to the death of my boyfriend, to the worth of the killer and the killed, respectively. I know now, Your Honor, that those who hear my voice turn the volume down in accordance with the worth they have assigned me.

"With little worth, I hold little power. And I have realized that power and empathy often have an inverse relationship. With more power, one loses empathy toward those with less.

"Your Honor, you and I can defy this norm." Tears prick my eyes, and my throat constricts. "Please, Your Honor, *we must*. Your power far exceeds ours, but this doesn't mean your empathy for us has to dissolve. Because, at the end of the day, you and my father are more alike than you are different. You're both brilliant men who love to read and need glasses to do so. You both have children you cherish and would do anything to protect. You both share those basic longings for love and respect and justice. You've both felt loneliness and the end of hope. You both know what it is to lose. And he has lost everything *twice.* Please, Your Honor, remember that though society has given you a higher worth than him, you are both human. So, I ask you to consider: if you were him, what sentence would you give yourself?"

I let out a shallow breath and say, "Thank you, Your Honor," before I return to my seat.

THIRTY-FOUR

Cal

MR. HAYES TOLD ME to not let Estlyn answer the door. I wonder if the LAPD threatening to break it down is what he had in mind when he said that. She bolts to stand, but I grab her arm. "I got it," I whisper as I push past her.

I swing open the door just as the officer again shouts, "LAPD. Open up!" There aren't one or two officers outside. There is a SWAT team crowding the hallway. My head snaps to Estlyn, whose shaking hands are raised above either side of her head.

"Dillon Collins?" the female officer in front asks.

Estlyn's voice is small behind me. "Right here."

The officer behind her points a gun Estlyn's way as the lady cop steps into the apartment with handcuffs. "Dillon Collins, you are under arrest for embezzlement of public funds." She pulls her hands, one by one, behind her back and reads

Estlyn her rights.

Estlyn, surprisingly calm, yells over the chaos to Dean. "Call Bishop. His cell number is in my tablet." As they lead her out the door, she adds, "Don't be bitchy."

And just like that, she's gone.

The SWAT team charges in, guns drawn, and starts tearing through the apartment. What the hell are they even looking for? Dean's ear is already to his phone when he yells, "Excuse you! Where's your warrant?"

Another officer drops an envelope on the coffee table and announces, "For her apartment, car, emails, and electronics. That tablet she mentioned?"

Dean massages his forehead between his fingers and thumb as he murmurs, "Fuck. It's at my place."

"One of our officers will take you to get it."

And now Dean's gone.

A cop is questioning Rory in the kitchen, and he's sweating. A lot. Okay, what the fuck are they busting her for? She stole something? That doesn't make her dangerous. What's with the SWAT team?

"Sir?"

I turn to see the warrant-dropping officer ushering me to the door.

In the hallway, he asks, "What's your name?"

I take a breath and comb my hair back with

shaky fingers before answering, "Linus Calloway."

"And how do you know Ms. Collins?"

"I met her last week at a bar—Bentley's Dive. I work there. She was a customer."

"And do you know what she does for a living?"

"Some kind of lawyer, but she didn't tell me anything beyond that."

"Does the name 'After Twelve' mean anything to you?"

"No. Nothing."

"What about this?" She holds up a white business card with a black *(12)* printed on one side.

"Yeah. That's her business card."

"Does the name Theodore or Ted Monroe ring a bell?"

"No."

"What about Michael Bishop?"

"Well, Estlyn just said Bishop. Is that her lawyer?"

"Has she ever hired you as an independent contractor?"

"What? No, I'm a screenwriter. What would she hire me to do?"

"Go inside and collect your things." I nod and head for the door just as Rory exits in handcuffs.

THIRTY-FIVE

Estlyn

GETTING ARRESTED IS LIKE having an orgasm, but not as fun. Actually, it's not fun at all, but they have more in common than meets the eye. There's all this buildup before each.

Is it going to happen now?

Nope.

Then another intense moment sneaks up on me and I think it might happen, but...

No, again.

Then...

Finally, it happens. The mystery of *when* is solved, and there's lots of chaos and mess and sometimes screaming, but afterward there's relief. I wasn't expecting to feel this relaxed, this calm when they pushed me into the back of the police car. Sure, I'm caught. I'll probably have to spend the prime of my life behind bars like a dangerous animal. But, hey, I took Monroe down with me.

And Rory.

I know they arrested him. The cop imploring me to waive my Fifth-Amendment right is about to burst a vein trying to convince me that Rory is ratting me out. God, I hope he is. *Take the fucking deal, Rory.* Always take the deal.

What no officer has explained is how the LAPD caught us. My guess: Monroe presented his list of suspects to a friend on the force after I rejected him. From there, it didn't take them long to narrow down means, motive, opportunity, and that essential *fuck the police, I got nuttin' to lose* attitude required to commit such a stupid crime. Of course, that ruled out all of Michael's upper-class, law-abiding family and left the mad-as-hell foster kid and her orphaned, computer geek of a teenage brother.

And, sure, it's possible they have insufficient evidence against us, in which case I could stay silent until arraignment, where I'll call their bluff. But that still won't stop Monroe from taking recompense into his own hands. Beyond a reasonable doubt or not, he believes Rory and I are the ones who wronged him.

Right now, they're leaving me alone to stew, which is the best they can do because I haven't said one word since I got here. When a suit stands in front of the door window, I assume it's Bishop. I feel awful for getting him out of bed or, possibly, out of the office. Let's be real—the office. He could have waited until tomorrow. It's not like I sleep at home. A cot in a cell is fine for the night.

But he isn't the suit that walks through the door.

THIRTY-SIX

Estlyn

FIVE YEARS AGO

I REINFORCE THE TWELFTH box of books with packing tape before looking for a new box to fill. When Michael and I moved into this apartment, we realized we were both book hoarders—me of fiction and poetry, him of philosophy and history. We filled the one floor-to-almost-ceiling bookcase we purchased within the first hour of unpacking. Then we looked at each other, at the shelves bowing under the weight of our collection, then at the handful of boxes of books left to find a home in our apartment. Without a word, he grabbed his wallet, tossed me my keys, and we headed to IKEA for another bookcase.

Rory is taking apart that second bookcase now. Michael's parents and brothers are packing up the kitchen and living room, taking carloads to their house, where I'll stay my senior year. I'd say I'm moving in with them because they are closer to campus than my parents, but I'm not. I'm moving in with them because they lost who

I did. I'm moving in with them because they understand something that my parents won't, even when they try. I'm moving in with them because Michael's mama holds me when I cry over an unwashed shirt that still smells like him, and she doesn't ask me to explain a thing.

I'm too damn worn out to explain myself.

His family knows I can't handle the media coverage, or lack thereof. They understand why I threw my phone when I read the article quoting the one black guy who supported Monroe walking free after killing Michael. My parents lost me when they told me: *try to understand how scared the officer was for his life. He thought he was pulling a gun on him. It was an honest mistake.*

What about how scared Michael was for his? How scared we all are? Would it have been an honest mistake if Michael had shot Officer Monroe four times? Because I can assure them, Michael was more scared for his life than Monroe was for his. And no one would have excused that *honest mistake.*

Officer Monroe will never convince me that he was truthful in his Internal Affairs interview. I won't believe that he thought his life was in danger, that Michael would have his gun out to shoot him before he did. I don't buy his explanation of why he chose to shoot instead use a taser at such close range. He can present his argument for why he thought Michael's life should have ended that second, but Monroe and I both know it's a line of reasoning he invented after the fact. Because there was no reasoning that night. There was only fear.

Fear. It's how all of us justify what happened at that traffic stop. But fear and reason can't overlap. Fear isn't higher-level thinking. It isn't logical. It's primal. It's a response so basic, every animal has it. And crucially, it's the fire that tests the deepest beliefs, reveals the truest character of the human species.

Not that fear is wrong. It isn't something to blame anyone for. Just like anger or jealousy or sadness, it springs forth from a place in the mind no one can control. But anger doesn't excuse violence. Jealousy doesn't excuse abuse. Sadness doesn't excuse self-destruction. And fear will never excuse the four bullets that killed Michael.

So, yes, Mom and Dad, I do understand. I understand more than they do because they won't stare down their own fear long enough to crush it. Because they're too ashamed to admit their fear of men like Michael, men like my dad, men whose skin is darker than their daughter's. They shouldn't be ashamed that they're afraid. They should be ashamed for pretending they aren't.

Rory's here because he gets it. Maybe because he's known me longer, or maybe because there's something about going through foster care that changes your idea of justice and what you have to do to get it. So when I told him my plan to put Monroe in prison for a lesser felony, he was eager to help. Or flaunt his computer-hacking skills with the challenge of breaking into the LAPD's system. It's a coin toss. Either way, Monroe was indicted this time for embezzling money from the force.

The justice system, motherfuckers.

I'm halfway done packing up the first bookshelf when I finally get to Michael's textbooks—almost all of which he refused to rent, then refused to part with when his course ended. I pull out an LSAT study guide. The binding is falling apart, the corners of the pages are frayed and fanned. I flip through it, trying to understand why Michael would keep it after he got a 174 on the exam, after UCLA accepted him.

In the margin above the introduction section is a paragraph in his handwriting. My heart halts when I see it's addressed to me.

Dillon,

I knew you'd come around. I'd say I'm not one for "I told you so," but I absolutely am. I told you so. You're going to make an incredible lawyer. I knew it that day in debate class, and these past couple years have confirmed that you are great at arguing and seem to enjoy it (at least with me).

You'll also probably score higher than I did on the LSAT because you're an obnoxious one-upper.

You remember how hard studying for the LSAT and applying for school was for me. Well, for both of us. It's draining and frustrating and like swimming through Jell-O some days. But you must keep at it. You must keep going. The world needs someone as brilliant and passionate as you to fight for them. I'll be here for you on the days you triumph and on those you feel like giving up.

I love you, baby.
Michael

Ps. "All persons ought to endeavor to follow what is right, and not what is established." Aristotle. Enough said.

My eyes shut as I finger the indents his words left on the page. His hand wrote these. His mind thought these. His heart pressed them here for me.

I'll be here for you.

I gather the rest of the LSAT study aids from the shelf and stack them beside me before I continue loading up the box with textbooks.

He will be here.

THIRTY-SEVEN

Estlyn

WELL, WELL, IF IT isn't the hypocrite DDA in the flesh, Rafael Ramirez, walking into my interrogation room. To refresh, he referred Ms. Sanchez to me when he failed to get justice for Mia in the Taylor East case. And now, he's my prosecutor. In jail or not, it's always nice to look down on others from the moral high ground.

"Ms. Collins, it's a pleasure." He offers his hand and a warm smile. I lift my wrists, cuffed to the table, in response. He sucks in an appalled breath, then yells out the door, "Sergeant Jackson, why the hell is Ms. Collins cuffed? Give me the key!" Ramirez shakes his head with apparent disgust as he unlocks my handcuffs. He pulls the chair across from me out from the table and sits. "I apologize for that. Are you hungry? Thirsty?"

I relax my freed hands in my lap and give him no reply.

"Your attorney is on his way, but I was hoping we could have a little chat, Bruin to Bruin, before he gets here."

Oh, sure, since you went to the same law school I did, by all means, let me incriminate myself. Reclining in my chair, I cross my arms over my chest.

"In my office. No cuffs. No police."

I raise my eyebrow before I break my silence. "No charges?"

Grinning, he folds his hands on the table. "Depends how our chat goes."

What the hell is this? Does he want me to fuck him or something? He should be so lucky. Although, I'd probably fuck him if it meant Rory didn't have to go to jail. Not because I'm a whore, because I'm a good sister.

Never mind. Just... no fucking. There are a million other ways to get Rory out of this, and when I finally think of one, I'll go that direction instead.

"I'd love to," I simper, "but I'd appreciate a third party. Wouldn't want to give anyone the wrong impression, now, would we?"

"Of course." Ramirez stands, opens the door, and waits patiently for me to let myself out. His hand steering my arm, we walk toward the door with the red exit light above it. I steal a glimpse into the other interrogation room. It's empty.

Without objection from a single officer, the DDA leads me through the lobby and out the front door, where a black SUV is waiting. The driver opens the back-seat door for us and helps me step up into the vehicle. I doubt we drive more than a mile to Ramirez's office building, which, despite the power he's attempting to exude, is unimpressive at best.

When we arrive at his office, a pantsuited woman and a man I immediately recognize as the Los Angeles District Attorney, Gavin Young, are waiting for us. Suddenly, I feel underdressed in my sweats and cropped tee. Hey, is it my fault I didn't know I was going to be arrested late at night and taken to some hostage-style meeting with LA's elite prosecutors?

"Gavin Young. Wonderful to meet you, Ms. Collins," Young says as he extends his hand to me. "Do you prefer Dillon or Estlyn? Or is it Zoe?"

Ha! Ramirez was eavesdropping on my meeting with Sanchez. I'll pat myself on the back later. "Estlyn is fine."

The woman beside him introduces herself as Emerson Brammer. That's all. No title. No context. Ramirez pulls a seat in front of the desk out for me. That's when I finally notice that we aren't in his office, but in Young's.

The DA sits and starts, "Please forgive the show of force tonight. Believe me when I say I wish this could have been handled any other way." He kicks his feet onto his desk and folds his hands over his gut. "Ramirez spoke highly of you, said the clients he sent your way were always pleased with your results."

Clients? Plural?

"And, when you got us another shot at Taylor East within a month of his acquittal, Emmy convinced me it was time to pull the trigger."

Who's Emmy?

Ladysuit chimes in, "As I'm sure you're aware, Young was nominated for governor in the primaries last week."

"Congratulations." Sure, I'm above fucking, but I'm not above ass-kissing.

Ladysuit again, "We want to hire After Twelve to work the campaign. More specifically, to make the poll numbers of Young's opponent, Alec Sellards, take a nosedive. We would have reached out via email, but, let's face it, no one wants a paper trail."

Speak for yourself. God knows I'd love a paper trail of leverage against the Los Angeles DA.

"If you get us in touch with your boss," Ladysuit concludes, "we'd be much obliged."

"And," Young adds, "if Samson agrees to work for us, I can make those little embezzlement charges disappear. For you and, of course, Rory."

I blow out my breath as my eyes scan each of their faces. "How much do y'all know about Samson?"

Young and Brammer turn to Ramirez, who kicks his foot from his opposite knee to the floor. He straightens up and starts, "Samson is an alias, obviously."

Ha. Obviously: a word uncertain people use to bolster the credibility of their bullshit.

"With the type of connections he appears to have," Ramirez goes on, "we've deduced that he's a high-ranking law enforcement officer—probably a captain, likely in the LAPD."

"Okay." I nod. "You should know that Samson is effective to be sure, but he's also…" I tilt my head from shoulder to shoulder while I decide how to continue, "…volatile. An arsonist and a mass murderer. Oh, and he has no qualms about killing with his bare hands or bludgeoning a man to death. Shall I go on?"

The inferiors look to Young. He responds with a hesitant nod.

"He also died thousands of years ago in a murder-suicide."

Young's eyebrow raises. "Excuse me?"

"He was a judge in the Bible. And a muse for Jeff Buckley. The *badass* of ancient revenge, don't you think?"

Suddenly sweating, Ramirez confirms, "So… there is no Samson."

With both index fingers, I point to myself. "Nice to meet you. And yes, I would like to take your case if we can agree to a few terms."

"Hold on," Young interrupts, "who do you work for, then?"

"Bitch, you think I need a boss?" Apparently,

that's my breaking point. Or two seconds ago, to be more precise.

"Terms," Brammer jumps in to de-escalate the rising tension. "What did you have in mind?"

"First, yes, you *will* expunge my record and Rory's. You will also make a public statement saying that Ted Monroe was not framed and that the alleged embezzlement was part of an undercover operation. Because of lack of interdepartmental communication, an error occurred that wrongfully incriminated him. You will also restore his full pension, whatever he would have gotten had he worked until retirement and not been arrested. But you *will not* give him his job back."

Young puts his hands out to stop me. "That's absurd. You're asking us to make the LAPD look *completely* incompetent."

"I'm asking you to protect your asset," I say as I gesture to myself. "Monroe is desperate to avenge himself. Give him the justice he doesn't deserve. That should satisfy him enough to get him to back off."

"Fine. We'll keep you safe from Monroe. Now," Young says as he passes me a document, "we have this NDA—"

I hold up a finger. "I'm not finished."

He sets the thick document in front of him and listens.

"I usually require a fifty-percent deposit up-front, but since this case will span the next five months, I'm willing to accept a retainer and bill by the hour instead."

Young smirks and sneaks a reaffirming glance at Ramirez. "Ms. Collins, my campaign is not going to pay you."

I shrug. "Your personal funds will suffice."

"The LAPD is in the process of seizing all of your assets. Your apartment is currently being torn apart by a dozen officers. Your car was impounded this evening. And," he grins through his patronizing tone, "let's not forget the delicate position you and your brother are in. Now, we'd be happy to return all of your belongings and your home with your cooperation."

"Oh..." I flip my black curls to my right shoulder then cross my arms, "so you want to en*slave* me. And if I refuse, you're going to incarcerate me." Young and I stare each other down. *That's right. Answer that, motherfucker.*

"You understand that we can't justify this as campaign spending."

"With all due respect, sir, you can justify it as legal counsel. I will be compensated."

"Fifty an hour."

"You pay your nanny more than that. Certainly, you care more about this campaign than your children."

"Fifty an hour or four years in prison and a felony on your record. Your choice."

"Two-fifty." I can make rent with that fee.

He huffs. "Emmy, include Ms. Collins's terms in her contract." Brammer nods and taps on her phone.

Oh, Emmy. Like Emerson. So, they're sleeping together. Young hands that nondisclosure my way again. This time I skim and sign it. It includes a line that states I cannot even admit to signing a gag order. I get it. This meeting and all subsequent ones did not and will not happen.

"And here's your phone," Young says as I exchange the NDA for a burner. "We will contact you on this to schedule our first meeting."

"Do my brother and I get to go home now?"

Young nods, and *Emmy* walks me to the door. "I'll show you to the car. Would you like us to pick your brother up from the station?"

"Yes." My feet straddle the threshold before I spin around. "Mr. Young?"

He buttons his coat and nods for me to continue.

"When I get you elected governor, you're going pardon an inmate named Alexander Hayes. He's fourteen years into a twenty-five-year sentence at the state prison in Lancaster for a crime he didn't commit."

"Ms. Collins, I can't just hand out a 'Get Out of Jail Free' card without at least looking into his case first."

I let out an audible sigh. "What a shame. I

wanted to give you a one-hundred-percent chance at winning, but—"

"Waive your fee, and I'll do it, no questions asked."

I don't need any time to think. "Deal."

THIRTY-EIGHT

Estlyn

FIVE YEARS AGO

"**OF COURSE,**" **I SPEAK** into the phone. This is my second week working Michael's old internship at Bishop and Colburn, and holy shit, there's a steep learning curve. I'm just a lowly intern, running copies and answering the phone, but it's like high-stakes running copies and answering the phone. "I'll have him call you as soon as he's available."

Stephen Colburn, Uncle Will's partner, walks through the door, passing my desk on the way to his office. He doesn't ask me how I'm doing like he usually does. He doesn't even acknowledge me. He looks wounded, like he's returning from a battle he lost.

"Mr. Colburn, I was about to run out to get lunch. Can I get you anything?"

He drops his bag on the floor and flops back onto the leather couch in our reception area. "A beer. Or several."

Is he serious? Because I'm twenty and it's

noon on a Tuesday. I'm not sure how I'm supposed to go buy a case of beer without a fake ID. Which I don't have.

He cracks just enough of a smirk for me to know he's joking. "Lucille's. Ribs, garlic mashed potatoes, sweet tea."

Nodding, I jot down his order on a sticky note.

"They convicted him." He sighs and throws his tie to the side of his chest. "Jordan Rahal."

"Oh." I know Rahal—the Syrian immigrant accused of breaking into a woman's apartment and raping her while wearing a condom, gloves, and a mask. DNA couldn't place him there. Only his cell's GPS could. But he also worked in the shop at the bottom of the apartment complex. Circumstantial shit. Not to mention there were other cases of rapes with the same pattern that our client couldn't have committed. "I'm sorry."

"I told him not to take the plea deal. I told him I'd get him out of it. They're almost never innocent. But this guy... this guy was."

"Yeah," I sigh, "I know how that goes."

"Anyway, I need you to update his file, please."

"Of course."

He stands and picks his bag off the floor. "After ribs. Ribs are your first priority."

I smile. "Yes, sir."

I glimpse the database on my computer as I

grab my purse from the back of my chair, then stoop to add a note in Rahal's file to remind me to close it out.

But I can't. Because his case isn't closed. He didn't get justice. Justice is supposed to be blind, but those jurors weren't. I can't imagine they overlooked his olive skin, that color we associate with bombings and hijackings. I would wager good money they heard silent alarms in their minds when they saw his emails typed in Arabic and heard the accents of his wife and children. If justice were really blind, Mr. Rahal would be free.

If she were blind, my dad would be, too.

And Michael would be working here instead of me.

Before I can consider what I'm doing, I scribble his wife's phone number on the sticky note with Colburn's lunch order.

Once I'm in my car, I dial the number and hit the call icon. It goes to voicemail. I glance at the book of E. E. Cummings poetry in my passenger seat right before the tone cues me to leave my message. "Hi, Mrs. Rahal. My name is... Estlyn. I'm part of an organization called..."

What's a good name? Why the hell did I call her before I had a plan? Maybe *After*—? Okay, *After* something. *After* justice fails? *After* twelve people failed to give her husband the verdict he deserved?

"...After Twelve. We work to get justice for those who couldn't find it in the court system. If you're interested in our services, give me a call at this number."

On my way back to the office, Mrs. Rahal's number lights up my phone.

THIRTY-NINE

Cal

LAST CALL WILL BE any minute now, and last call means I have to go lie awake on Elliot's couch. I didn't go straight to his place from Estlyn's because I didn't want to hear about how shitty my taste in women is. Instead, I'm at the Dive, my cheek flat on my crossed arms, ignoring the girl who's been trying to talk to me for the last hour. *Fuck off, sexy serial killer. Or bank robber. Or Lecter-esque skin collector. I've had enough crazy.*

My elbow zings when my phone buzzes the table beneath it. I lift my head to see Estlyn's number. I shouldn't answer, but my fingers do before I can stop them. "Hello?"

"Linus! Hey, I'm so sorry about earlier."

"No, that's okay." Except it *so* is not.

"It was a mistake. They let us go."

Really? Do innocent people put their hands up when the cops knock on their door? She looked guilty as sin to me.

"I know it looked bad, but do you remember

hearing about the police shooting five years ago? Michael Bishop, the guy in his car that that Officer Monroe gunned down?"

Can she read my mind? "No, I don't remember that. But the cops asked me if I knew those names tonight."

"Well, I was in the car when Monroe shot Michael. So, I—"

"Shit, Est, I'm so sorry."

"It's fine," she snaps.

Okay, apparently that's a touchy subject.

"Just wanted to explain why I was so quick to give myself up. There aren't a lot of options when a cop points a gun at you, right?"

"Yeah."

"Anyway, I'm home now. It's a disaster, but I'm home."

"God, I'm so relieved. Rory's home, too?"

"Yeah."

A long pause lingers between us. I was supposed to stay with her tonight. Is she going to invite me? Or do I need to invite myself?

"Can I—"

"Do you—" we both start. She snickers. "You go."

"Oh, just wanted to know if I should come back."

"Linus, who else is going to clean up this mess?"

I grin like an idiot and answer, "I'll add it to

your bill. See you in ten."

"Thanks, Linus."

ESTLYN COLLAPSED INTO BED around four this morning. It's one o'clock now, and, as far as I know, she hasn't moved from her stomach or her drool pool once. I woke up at ten and have checked her pulse three times since. She's still alive, just sleeping for real for once. I placed Lioness on the pillow in front of her face so Estlyn will have company when she wakes up.

After the chaos of last night, I've taken the morning (midday?) to chill on the balcony with one of the books Estlyn bought. I've just found out that the crazy girlfriend of the teenage murderer is pregnant when my phone buzzes with a text from Elliot:

Your dad's an asshole.

That's not news to me, but okay. I open the link to some Hollywood gossip article Elliot included. Its title: "*Calloway Denies Allegations of Sexual Misconduct.*" All I can think is how uncreative that title is. But, this power abuse happens so often, those poor journalists probably get just as tired of it all as we do. I can picture the editor saying, *Ah, fuck it, that bland title is fine. It's not like we can write Calloway is a Lying Prick of a Man-Whore without getting hit with a defamation suit.*

Anyway, the article reads:

Ron Calloway finally breaks his silence after actress Erin Kennedy accused him of coercing her to have sex with him in exchange for a role on his series When We Fall. Calloway responded Friday, unilaterally denying Kennedy's claims. "Yes, Erin and I did have a sexual relationship," he said in a statement through his lawyer, "but it was consensual. She has long been a friend of my family, and it is unthinkable that I would abuse my power to hurt someone so dear to me." Calloway went on to try to discredit Kennedy's claims, saying he was the victim of blackmail. "The day before Erin's story broke, Zoe Whitaker from After Twelve tried to extort me into firing Taylor East. When I refused, Whitaker messaged me, 'Enjoy the TMZ headline with your name in it.'"

After Twelve is an underground, revenge-for-hire service. However, claims of its existence have yet to be substantiated."

Holy shit.

I step back into the apartment and find my wallet on the kitchen counter. The business card Estlyn left on the bar the night we met is still in here. I pull it out to see the printed *(12)* surrounded by the E. E. Cummings lines she wrote. I flip it over to find the email address on the back: *samson@aftertwelve.com*.

The events of the last couple of weeks fall together like pieces of a puzzle.

I slept with Estlyn.

Dean approached Erin for a story about my dad a day or two after.

The story that Estlyn told Dean to pursue.

The story about my ex and my dad.

Estlyn didn't pick some guy up at a bar. She picked up leverage.

I look through the open bedroom door at Estlyn, lost in peaceful slumber.

Manipulative. Little. Bitch.

ABOUT THE AUTHOR

 Growing up with poor reading comprehension, Laney Wylde avoided books at all costs. But after reading Francine River's Redeeming Love for the first time in high school, she fell in love with literature. It was then she realized broken anti-heroines and impossible love stories were the stuff of heart-wrenching, binge-worthy novels.

Afraid her slow reading pace and lack of writing skill would inhibit her from becoming a successful English major, Laney pursued her B.S. in Mathematics from Biola University, graduating in 2014.

Laney gathered the courage to write honestly and diligently in 2017, producing Never Touched, a passion project that sheds light on the uphill battle that is healing from sexual abuse.

She lives in Southern California with her dashing husband and precocious little boy.

ACKNOWLEDGEMENTS

THIS SERIES WOULD HAVE never had happened without my husband. Thank you, E, for picking me up when I fell down, for saying, "Obviously, people would read that," when I pitched you the idea of a female lead who ruined people's lives for a living, for listening to my "Wah, wah, I'll never write again," and loving me anyway.

My MoFos. Whitney, between you and me, I believe your word over all the others. Stacey, we both know I'm too insecure to write without your constant affirmation. Therefore, you're basically responsible for all my books. Sarah, thank you for reading while feeding your baby in the middle of the night and doing all my amazing graphics. You're a super hero. Lizzie, thank you for saying, "Yeah, white girl, you can't write that," after reading parts of my book. Also, make sure I'm on Cameron's list for when you and E die.

On that note, Cameron, Kaylie, and Lizzie, thank you for answering all my insensitive questions about being black in the United States. Thank you for recommending books, documentaries, podcasts, and telling me about black girl hair. I couldn't have written this without you!

Michelle Alexander, you don't know me, but your book, The New Jim Crow, changed how I read the news, think and talk about race, and watch TV. I hope I get to meet you some day. For your sake, I hope I don't because I'm pretty weird when I fan girl over people.

To my girls at CTP, thank you for taking on this series of mine. I love working with you all!

Last, I'm grateful for God's grace. I'm not sure why you've given the opportunity to have my dream job, but thank you.